Samuel French Acting Edition

M000307789

Homos,
or Everyone in America

by Jordan Seavey

SAMUELFRENCH.COM   SAMUELFRENCH.CO.UK

For Production Enquiries

United States and Canada
Info@SamuelFrench.com
1-866-598-8449

United Kingdom and Europe
Plays@SamuelFrench.co.uk
020-7255-4302

Each title is subject to availability from Samuel French, depending upon country of performance. Please be aware that *HOMOS, OR EVERYONE IN AMERICA* may not be licensed by Samuel French in your territory. Professional and amateur producers should contact the nearest Samuel French office or licensing partner to verify availability.

MUSIC USE NOTE

Licensees are solely responsible for obtaining formal written permission from copyright owners to use copyrighted music in the performance of this play and are strongly cautioned to do so. If no such permission is obtained by the licensee, then the licensee must use only original music that the licensee owns and controls. Licensees are solely responsible and liable for all music clearances and shall indemnify the copyright owners of the play(s) and their licensing agent, Samuel French, against any costs, expenses, losses and liabilities arising from the use of music by licensees. Please contact the appropriate music licensing authority in your territory for the rights to any incidental music.

IMPORTANT BILLING AND CREDIT REQUIREMENTS

If you have obtained performance rights to this title, please refer to your licensing agreement for important billing and credit requirements.

HOMOS, OR EVERYONE IN AMERICA was originally produced by Labyrinth Theater Company (Mimi O'Donnell, Artistic Director; Danny Feldman, Managing Director) at the Bank Street Theater, New York, October 20 through December 11, 2016. The production was directed by Mike Donahue, with sets by Dane Laffrey, lighting by Scott Zielinski, costumes by Jessica Pabst, and original composition and sound by Daniel Kluger and Lee Kinney. The Production Stage Manager was Hannah Woodward, and the Assistant Stage Manager was Lily Perlmutter. *Homos, or Everyone in America* was developed, in part, with assistance from The Orchard Project, a program of The Exchange (www.exchangenyc.org), and also received support from the New York Theatre Workshop Annual Usual Suspects Summer Residency at Dartmouth College. The cast was as follows:

THE WRITER	Michael Urie
THE ACADEMIC	Robin De Jesús
DAN	Aaron Costa Ganis
LAILA	Stacey Sargeant

CHARACTERS

THE WRITER – male, caucasian jew, ages from late twenties to early thirties
THE ACADEMIC – male, latino, ages from late twenties to early thirties
DAN – a friend, male, race: he's adopted so who knows? thirty-ish
LAILA – a stranger, female, any race but caucasian, thirty-ish

SETTING

brooklyn, new york

TIME

moments scattered throughout 2006-2011
(NOTE: in production, this should be included in audience programs:
"the play takes place in brooklyn, new york, jumping around in
moments scattered throughout 2006-2011")

AUTHOR'S NOTES

"–" means silence, waiting, and/or a significant shift in thought,
intention, and/or action

the space is probably empty, or mostly so

think "intimate" – it's okay if the actors and the audience are in each
other's laps

probably few or even no props

the dates that accompany each scene are chronological signposts for the
artistic team but should not be projected or otherwise shared with the
audience in production

Dedicated, with love, to Barie Shortell

"We hear music better at night, did you know that? Because of from when we used to have to listen for the sound of some animal coming out of the dark to kill us by our little fires. So music sounds better when it's dark. Music. Because we're listening for our murderer. A shaggy animal with a thirst for blood, a hunger for muscle and bone, lurking somewhere in the bushes and notes."

from *Tragedy: A Tragedy* by Will Eno

The Lush Soap Store (Part 1)
February 16, 2011

LAILA.

but they do explode with glitter

and this one with salts and perfumes

and this one with real dried lavender

THE WRITER.

neat

water's the detonator

LAILA.

the detonator

THE WRITER.

when you drop the bath bomb in the water

LAILA.

ohhhhh

yes of course

water's the detonator

so

is it for a special occasion

or for anyone in particular

orrrrr

THE WRITER.

what

LAILA.

for that special someone

The First Date (Part 1)
April 21, 2006

> (**THE WRITER** *and* **THE ACADEMIC** *at the wine
> bar.*)

THE ACADEMIC.

red

THE WRITER.

red

–

–

white

–

–

red

–

uh

white

sorry

uh sorry

no

no

yes

sorry

white

definitely white

definitely white

yes

definitely white

THE ACADEMIC.

white

THE WRITER.

wait

sorry

red

sorry

red

yes

red

red

sorry

THE ACADEMIC.

red

THE WRITER.

yes

red

wait

sorry ummm

mmmmmmmmmmmmm

wellll

white

sorry

white

THE ACADEMIC.

yes

THE WRITER.

oh yes

white

THE ACADEMIC.

white

THE WRITER.

white

oh yeah

white

for sure

THE ACADEMIC.

white then

THE WRITER.
  white

THE ACADEMIC.
  white

  —

  —

  —

THE WRITER.
  red

The First Talk About Monogamy
January 22, 2007

THE WRITER.

never

THE ACADEMIC.

nope

THE WRITER.

really

THE ACADEMIC.

i mean never

say never

right

THE WRITER.

stupid fucking phrase though

never

say never

stupid

THE ACADEMIC.

right but so i

THE WRITER.

fucking phrase

THE ACADEMIC.

hesitate to say never

because i have a policy

a creed

THE WRITER.

a dictum

THE ACADEMIC.

yes a

what

THE WRITER.

a dictum

—

THE ACADEMIC.
    right
    a dictum
    to never say never
    so i never
    (wah wah)
    do

THE WRITER.
    zing

THE ACADEMIC.
    wasn't terribly funny
    but you did say "dictum"

THE WRITER.
    i did

THE ACADEMIC.
    dictum

THE WRITER.
    you're four

THE ACADEMIC.
    five

THE WRITER.
    years old

THE ACADEMIC.
    i know
    but back to

THE WRITER.
    dictum

THE ACADEMIC.
    shut up
    i wanna

THE WRITER.
    dictum

THE ACADEMIC.
    i'm being serious

i don't think it's my

my

THE WRITER.

dictum

THE ACADEMIC.

thing

–

do you

i mean

do you want to

THE WRITER.

i mean

no

i mean

–

no

THE ACADEMIC.

have you had one

before

THE WRITER.

several but

THE ACADEMIC.

oh

wow

several

THE WRITER.

well

um

yeah

THE ACADEMIC.

with your ex

THE WRITER.

no

no never

no just like

THE ACADEMIC.

what

THE WRITER.

the single life

livin la vida loca

THE ACADEMIC.

of course

THE WRITER.

at the bachelor pad

back when i was a

you know

THE ACADEMIC.

right

THE WRITER.

bachelor

but i mean

i wouldn't

rule it out

—

would

would you

THE ACADEMIC.

i

i don't know

to be honest

THE WRITER.

right i under

you know

stand

THE ACADEMIC.

i don't feel the need to

the need for

THE WRITER.
    well it's not like i need
    it's not like i'm
    un

THE ACADEMIC.
    un

THE WRITER.
    unhappy
    or un
    un

THE ACADEMIC.
    satisfied

THE WRITER.
    or unsatisfied

THE ACADEMIC.
    okay good

THE WRITER.
    per se
    –

THE ACADEMIC.
    per se
    what do you

THE WRITER.
    no no i only mean i
    listen
    i'm just open
    open minded

THE ACADEMIC.
    i'm more like potentially

THE WRITER.
    potentially

THE ACADEMIC.
    you're not gonna like this word

tolerant

THE WRITER.

tolerant

ugh i haaaaate

THE ACADEMIC.

no no no

THE WRITER.

that word

THE ACADEMIC.

listen

you know me

you know i'm open minded too

THE WRITER.

and i love that

THE ACADEMIC.

thanks

THE WRITER.

about you

THE ACADEMIC.

yeah and you also like my

THE WRITER.

what

THE ACADEMIC.

dictum

THE WRITER.

i do like your dictum

THE ACADEMIC.

nor do i think i'm

antiquated

THE WRITER.

never

THE ACADEMIC.

or unmalleable

THE WRITER.
never
THE ACADEMIC.
because compromise is
THE WRITER.
always
THE ACADEMIC.
but
i don't think i'd be comfortable
sharing you
THE WRITER.
sharing me
i am not a sweater
THE ACADEMIC.
no i mean
THE WRITER.
or a
a plate of ribs
THE ACADEMIC.
i didn't mean
THE WRITER.
or even an anecdote
THE ACADEMIC.
i know you are not an anecdote
THE WRITER.
it's something we'd share
together
THE ACADEMIC.
you mean someone
someone we'd
THE WRITER.
but emotionally it wouldn't
THE ACADEMIC.
right

right

theoretically

right

–

but anyway

why are we even

THE WRITER.

we're not

it's hypothetical

but heeeeey

just remember your

THE ACADEMIC.

what

THE WRITER.

dictum

THE ACADEMIC.

ah

THE WRITER.

never

say never

THE ACADEMIC.

never

The Night The Street Lights Went Dark (Part 1)
June 9, 2006

(Sleep. Deep silence. **THE ACADEMIC** *bolts awake.)*

THE ACADEMIC.

babe

babe wake up

THE WRITER.

what

what is it

THE ACADEMIC.

did you hear

you didn't hear anything

THE WRITER.

hear

no i was asleep

our argument about poppers earlier this evening

totally tuckered

THE ACADEMIC.

i heard

THE WRITER.

me out

THE ACADEMIC.

swear i heard

thought i heard

THE WRITER.

someone

here

THE ACADEMIC.

i

i guess not

but

*(***THE ACADEMIC** *goes to a window.)*

what in the

have you seen this

did you know the lights are all

THE WRITER.

lights

THE ACADEMIC.

the street lights

the whole block

they're all

THE WRITER.

what

THE ACADEMIC.

dark

what in the

THE WRITER.

i'm sure it's just

THE ACADEMIC.

world

THE WRITER.

an outage

these things

THE ACADEMIC.

so strange

THE WRITER.

happen from time to

THE ACADEMIC.

i've never

THE WRITER.

time

worse comes to worst

it's the taliban

THE ACADEMIC.

swear i heard a

THE WRITER.
in which case

THE ACADEMIC.
my heart is
my pulse

THE WRITER.
who cares
we'll all be

THE ACADEMIC.
the hairs on my

THE WRITER.
dead anyway so

THE ACADEMIC.
god you are so morbid

THE WRITER.
i say enjoy the

THE ACADEMIC.
even in the middle of the

THE WRITER.
dark

THE ACADEMIC.
night

THE WRITER.
enjoy the dark
while we've

THE ACADEMIC.
i will never

THE WRITER.
got it

THE ACADEMIC.
sleep

–

THE WRITER.
shhh

shhhhh
here
i'll put on some
vivaldi
or maybe

THE ACADEMIC.

no no
vivaldi is good

THE WRITER.

vivaldi is good
vivaldi it is then

  (Vivaldi plays. They listen.)

THE ACADEMIC.

but i'll never sleep
i'm serious
i hate the dark being this dark
why do you think i live in new york

  (Listening. **THE ACADEMIC** *tosses and turns.)*

i will never sleep

THE WRITER.

shhhh
just listen

The First Date (Part 2)
April 21, 2006

THE ACADEMIC.
one more round
THE WRITER.
but me drunk drunk
THE ACADEMIC.
two more please
life
THE WRITER.
you
THE ACADEMIC.
is for living
THE WRITER.
are trouble

–

THE ACADEMIC.
so you're a
a um
THE WRITER.
oh
THE ACADEMIC.
writer
THE WRITER.
oh are we
i write
yes
THE ACADEMIC.
right
so doesn't that
THE WRITER.
right

THE ACADEMIC.

make you a

THE WRITER.

right

THE ACADEMIC.

writer

THE WRITER.

i don't know what makes a

a writer a writer

it's a very formal

THE ACADEMIC.

oh

THE WRITER.

term

THE ACADEMIC.

right

title

THE WRITER.

label

and i don't

you know

THE ACADEMIC.

no

THE WRITER.

have a master's in

which has become increasingly

uhhh

THE ACADEMIC.

necessary

THE WRITER.

in vogue

THE ACADEMIC.

vogue

vogue

–

THE WRITER.

here's to

um

madonna

THE ACADEMIC.

or us

THE WRITER.

oh

duh

to us

–

but so anyway

you

you're getting your

THE ACADEMIC.

comeuppance

THE WRITER.

i meant your master's

THE ACADEMIC.

same thing

THE WRITER.

buh dum bum

THE ACADEMIC.

oh you are so

THE WRITER.

what

THE ACADEMIC.

cute

THE WRITER.

no

THE ACADEMIC.

when you make sounds

THE WRITER.

aw shucks

THE ACADEMIC.

onomatopoeic

THE WRITER.

ahhhmmm

THE ACADEMIC.

sounds

–

THE WRITER.

but so you're getting your master's in

in

THE ACADEMIC.

media studies

THE WRITER.

media studies

awesome

THE ACADEMIC.

thanks

THE WRITER.

um what are media studies

am i dumb

i am dumb

is it the study of

um

media

THE ACADEMIC.

you would think

THE WRITER.

yes but i'm dumb

THE ACADEMIC.

no

media studies

is made up

it's a new
well not new but
comparatively recent
in terms of
–
it's academic

THE WRITER.
please explain i'm drunk

THE ACADEMIC.
you lush

THE WRITER.
no i

THE ACADEMIC.
kidding
i come here a lot
so who's the lush
it's my favorite

THE WRITER.
it's nice
a wine bar

THE ACADEMIC.
so bougie i know

THE WRITER.
no no no it's
well yeah very but

THE ACADEMIC.
that's park slope

THE WRITER.
it's charming

THE ACADEMIC.
and pricey

THE WRITER.
guess they need whole bars
just for wine now

THE ACADEMIC.
    wine is life
    wine is blood

THE WRITER.
    i guess if there's demand

THE ACADEMIC.
    like jesus christ died for our

THE WRITER.
    park slope must supply
    oh
    are you religious

THE ACADEMIC.
    no
    recovering catholic

THE WRITER.
    ah
    yeah
    and it's not a dive bar or
    sports bar or
    too cruisey

THE ACADEMIC.
    right and not gay

THE WRITER.
    no not gay but
    what's the phrase

THE ACADEMIC.
    "mixed"

THE WRITER.
    mixed
    gays and straights
    mixed together
    ruh roh

THE ACADEMIC.
    look out

THE WRITER.

"gay friendly"

THE ACADEMIC.

as opposed to gay unfriendly

gay tolerant

THE WRITER.

ugh i haaaaate

THE ACADEMIC.

they tolerate us

THE WRITER.

that word

THE ACADEMIC.

"mixed" then

THE WRITER.

but not that mixed

THE ACADEMIC.

well it is park slope not christopher street

THE WRITER.

they should put a stroller park out front

baby's first chianti

THE ACADEMIC.

i wish to reprimand your stereotyping

but cannot

THE WRITER.

why

THE ACADEMIC.

they do

THE WRITER.

they serve babies wine here

THE ACADEMIC.

no

they open the front when it's warm

it turns into a baby patch

THE WRITER.

a white baby patch i bet

THE ACADEMIC.

relatively white

oh and weekends especially

like is this a bar or a nursery school

and let me tell you

mothers

drink

early

THE WRITER.

but aren't they all breast

THE ACADEMIC.

breastfeeding

doesn't stop them

well recent studies say

a little ethanol a day

keeps the doc

THE WRITER.

babies not gay

THE ACADEMIC.

yeah right

as if gays have trouble drinking

THE WRITER.

i did hear that about you specifically

THE ACADEMIC.

shut up

THE WRITER.

why do you think i agreed to meet up from

THE ACADEMIC.

oh god

THE WRITER.

friendster

THE ACADEMIC.

fucking friendster

THE WRITER.

hey it's a brave

THE ACADEMIC.

do you even think

THE WRITER.

new world

THE ACADEMIC.

friendster will

THE WRITER.

connection

THE ACADEMIC.

survive

THE WRITER.

connecting people

it's

THE ACADEMIC.

sustain its

THE WRITER.

kind of amazing if you

THE ACADEMIC.

because personally i think it's

THE WRITER.

because you and i would never have met if

THE ACADEMIC.

a fad

THE WRITER.

a fad

yeah right

everyone thought email was a fad

friendster's no fad

friendster is here to stay

THE ACADEMIC.
>i think friendster's an early and popular example
>of what's bound to be a sprawling lineage
>of internet based social networking websites which

THE WRITER.
>no no no
>friendster forever
>mark my words

THE ACADEMIC.
>yeah your slurred words
>sluuurrrds

THE WRITER.
>no i don't usually drink like
>well
>i didn't have my first drink
>till my twenty-first birthday

THE ACADEMIC.
>whaaaaaaaaaaaaaat

THE WRITER.
>well i was like this goody two shoes
>and so by college i was like
>"i don't need alcohol
>i don't need drugs to have a good

THE ACADEMIC.
>right

THE WRITER.
>time"

THE ACADEMIC.
>but it sure does help

THE WRITER.
>sure does
>and also
>my dad

THE ACADEMIC.

    oh

    is he a

THE WRITER.

    no

    but his dad was

    and actually my other grandfather was too so

    genetically i still worry and

THE ACADEMIC.

    right

THE WRITER.

    and so my dad never touched a

    he's a teetotaler

THE ACADEMIC.

    whoa

THE WRITER.

    well his dad walked out

    when he

    my dad

    was two

THE ACADEMIC.

    whoa

THE WRITER.

    years old

    so he

    my dad

    never touched a drop

THE ACADEMIC.

    never

THE WRITER.

    never

    i mean basically i come from a long line

    of alcoholics and compulsive gamblers

and yes i do use that line on every first date

THE ACADEMIC.

i'm hooked

THE WRITER.

anyway

so he

my dad

instilled some serious terror of the drink in me and

well

i would never raise a child that way

with such imposing you know

black and white absolutes

not to mention

you know

reagan

THE ACADEMIC.

reagan

THE WRITER.

didn't help that my dad's name is

THE ACADEMIC.

reagan

THE WRITER.

ronald

THE ACADEMIC.

ah

THE WRITER.

growing up in the eighties was

you know

it was a hijacked decade

i mean the challenger crash

the kool-aid in jonestown

g.i. joe: a real american hero

THE ACADEMIC.

smurfs

THE WRITER.
smurfs
and the war on drugs

THE ACADEMIC.
well nixon started that but

THE WRITER.
"mom nixon started it!"

THE ACADEMIC.
but at least it worked

THE WRITER.
oh it worked perfectly

THE ACADEMIC.
good job america

THE WRITER.
drug free

THE ACADEMIC.
just say no to

THE WRITER.
dare to keep kids off

THE ACADEMIC.
this is your brain on

Four Weeks After The Attack (Part 1)
March 15, 2011

THE ACADEMIC.

    it reminded me of that one summer night

    when we were first

    do you remember that one night

    all the street lights on my block went out that night

THE WRITER.

    yes

    and i thought it was the taliban

    but that not getting sleep

    was a scarier prospect

    so i put on vivaldi

THE ACADEMIC.

    i said i would never fall asleep

THE WRITER.

    but you did

    i put on vivaldi and you did fall asleep

THE ACADEMIC.

    he's a snooze

    but most of all

    i remember waking up that night and i know it sounds
    so silly but

    i could swear there was

    something

    next to the bed

    next to my ear

    breathing into it

    saying

    –

    gonna get you

    –

The Beach (Part 1)
August 12, 2007

(On the phone.)

THE WRITER.
you're still at the

THE ACADEMIC.
at the beach yeah
i'm
we're leaving soon
it's

THE WRITER.
"we're" leaving soon
you and
who are you with

THE ACADEMIC.
huh

THE WRITER.
who are you there with

THE ACADEMIC.
told you i ran into a

THE WRITER.
who

THE ACADEMIC.
my friend

THE WRITER.
which friend

THE ACADEMIC.
the one i met a few months back at
the friend from the school thing

THE WRITER.
school thing

THE ACADEMIC.
presentation

we have a bunch of mutual
whatever it doesn't matter i'm leaving soon it's

THE WRITER.

dan
the one you said was

THE ACADEMIC.

huh

THE WRITER.

oh i remember that conversation
handsome "sort of" strapping dan

–

can't believe you're still
you said leaving soon
then forty-five minutes later

THE ACADEMIC.

he
he went and cracked another beer
i couldn't

THE WRITER.

right of course
more beer

THE ACADEMIC.

acting like a jealous thirteen
no a twelve-year-old
it is so

THE WRITER.

i'm not jealous i'm

THE ACADEMIC.

immature

THE WRITER.

infuriated being told one thing
then forty-five minutes later it's a

THE ACADEMIC.

oh for god's sake it's summer

it's beautiful and a

THE WRITER.

whole other

THE ACADEMIC.

beach

THE WRITER.

story

THE ACADEMIC.

you know how time

time here just

THE WRITER.

you've known about this party since

THE ACADEMIC.

folds and stretches

doubles back

layers and

THE WRITER.

people are already arriving

people are already here

and you're

THE ACADEMIC.

i know i

i'm coming i'm

—

i'm sorry

i'm coming

The First Date (Part 3)
April 21, 2006

THE ACADEMIC.

    and if the bar slows by like 2:30

THE WRITER.

    wait is it already 2:30

THE ACADEMIC.

    2:45 actually

    so if the wine's flowing slower

    like tonight

    though i do want one last nightcap

    if there are just regulars left

    old fogies like me

THE WRITER.

    us

THE ACADEMIC.

    old fogies like us

    then they pull down the gate and

THE WRITER.

    oh fuuuuun

THE ACADEMIC.

    it turns into like a smoking den

THE WRITER.

    think i love park slope

THE ACADEMIC.

    you smoke

THE WRITER.

    cigarettes

    nah

THE ACADEMIC.

    no i meant

THE WRITER.

    oh

pot

oh yeah

i concede to the weed

if you know what i

THE ACADEMIC.

cool

wasn't sure just cause

THE WRITER.

first drink on my twenty-first

THE ACADEMIC.

right

THE WRITER.

nah that was 2001

those first few months

if i got tipsy i'd just start crying

THE ACADEMIC.

ruh roh

THE WRITER.

about 9/11

THE ACADEMIC.

awwwww

THE WRITER.

no it wasn't cute

my friends were like

"oh god y'all he's tipsy

here come the tears of 9/11"

(A joint is being passed around the bar.)

THE ACADEMIC.

so what should we smoke to

THE WRITER.

the war on drugs

THE ACADEMIC.

ronald reagan

THE WRITER.
    my dad
THE ACADEMIC.
    to your daaaad
THE WRITER.
    to my daaaaad
THE ACADEMIC.
    our fathers
THE WRITER.
    our forefathers
THE ACADEMIC.
    to abraham lincoln
THE WRITER.
    to the men in charge of us
THE ACADEMIC.
    no I'M in charge of
    i'm in charge of
THE WRITER.
    what
THE ACADEMIC.
    me
    i'm in charge of me
    and i am really glad we met tonight
THE WRITER.
    me too

    –

THE ACADEMIC.
    oh so media studies
    so it's not not the study of media
    that's true
    it is about the contentment of
    sorry
    the content of
    media

but more pointedly
it's about the history of media
the effects of media

THE WRITER.
interesting

THE ACADEMIC.
it's a lot of theory
there are like three branches
critique of aesthetic forms like um genre and narrative
then production of media
well not its production but the study of its production
then sociological analysis
like the effects on our population
and blah blah blah
it's a lot of theory it's

(**THE WRITER** *coughs violently.*)

THE WRITER.
wow this is strong
this weed is like
really strong

THE ACADEMIC.
you okay

THE WRITER.
toooootally
so it's like there's this one thing
media
and then there's this other·thing
study
and together they made a baby
a studious mediated baby
called media studies

THE ACADEMIC.
right but since we're like outside of media
not like making the media but like

    outside looking in

THE WRITER.

    judging

THE ACADEMIC.

    analyzing

THE WRITER.

    academiatizing

THE ACADEMIC.

    okay sure

    since we're all academiatizing

    once you get past its simple name

    it gets like silly complicated

    it's a lot of theory

    and theory is

THE WRITER.

    theoretical

THE ACADEMIC.

    well theoretically

    –

    anyway

    it's an exciting time in the field

    because there's so much new media

    the internet is changing everything and

THE WRITER.

    so you're getting your master's in friendster

THE ACADEMIC.

    oh you are just sooooo

THE WRITER.

    wasted

    i am schwasted

    that is all fact and no theory

    i'm founding the first schwasted studies program in
    america

THE ACADEMIC.

no

you are adorable

> (**THE ACADEMIC** *leans in to kiss* **THE WRITER**, *but doesn't because:*)

THE WRITER.

one sec

one sec

THE ACADEMIC.

oh

okay

is something

> (**THE WRITER** *runs outside. Vomiting, a lot of vomiting.* **THE ACADEMIC** *follows.*)

oh god

are you

THE WRITER.

oh god

no i'm

yeah i'm

totally fine

i am 100 percent fi

> (*Vomiting, more vomiting.*)

THE ACADEMIC.

oh no oh god

THE WRITER.

i'm sorry

i'm sorry

THE ACADEMIC.

no no no

do you need

can i get you

THE WRITER.

    oh no

    i'm good

    i am great

    just spinning

    and vomiting

THE ACADEMIC.

    here let me get you some

THE WRITER.

    no no no

    i am not fifteen

    years old

    the rodeo

    has been attended

    before

    all evidence to the

THE ACADEMIC.

    don't worry it's

THE WRITER.

    at least i'm not crying about 9/11

    because that would

      (Vomiting. More vomiting.)

The Beach (Part 2)
August 10, 2007

(THE ACADEMIC on the phone.)

THE ACADEMIC.

i'm sorry

i'm coming

—

you're not

it's my bad

i lost track of

listen i'm putting my bathing suit back on as we speak

so

—

no we are not at the nude beach

that was a joke

—

okay be there soon

i love

> *(THE WRITER has hung up. THE ACADEMIC hangs up.)*

you

DAN.

everything okay

THE ACADEMIC.

peachy

DAN.

actually why didn't we go to the nude beach

next time we should go to the

THE ACADEMIC.

yeah that'd be

DAN.

and bring yer boyfriend

we've never met and

THE ACADEMIC.
i'm sure you will

DAN.
you're not hiding him are you

THE ACADEMIC.
no no no
i mean
no
i'm not hiding him
he is great
but um
now i do really have to

DAN.
yeah yeah of course
i'm glad he's great
you are great too
great deserves great
oh and this was fun so
thanks

THE ACADEMIC.
yeah super nice

DAN.
for inviting me

THE ACADEMIC.
to have a beach buddy

DAN.
isn't that what having a boyfriend is for

THE ACADEMIC.
mine hates the beach

DAN.
who on earth could hate a beach

THE ACADEMIC.
i'll introduce you

DAN.

i'm jealous

THE ACADEMIC.

jealous

DAN.

singlehood is a fucking waking nightmare

i miss being boyfriended

THE ACADEMIC.

you can have mine

DAN.

i guess "the grass is always greener

THE ACADEMIC.

"take my boyfriend

DAN.

but you still gotta fuckin' mow it"

THE ACADEMIC.

please"

DAN.

you know who said that to me once

joan didion

THE ACADEMIC.

wait what

no

DAN.

yes

story for another

THE ACADEMIC.

you always have the best

DAN.

time

THE ACADEMIC.

stories

—

DAN.

hey

why'd you tell him you ran into me

THE ACADEMIC.

what do you

DAN.

you said you just "ran into" me at the

THE ACADEMIC.

no i

DAN.

beach

THE ACADEMIC.

didn't

did i

DAN.

yeah

i mean no big deal but

THE ACADEMIC.

hm i don't know

don't think i was thinking

blah blah blah just running my

DAN.

ah

THE ACADEMIC.

mouth

–

DAN.

your beer's still

half full

–

The Night The Street Lights Went Out (Part 2)
June 9, 2006

THE ACADEMIC.

do you

THE WRITER.

what

THE ACADEMIC.

think it's bad

THE WRITER.

what

THE ACADEMIC.

that we use poppers

THE WRITER.

no

THE ACADEMIC.

no

THE WRITER.

i mean it's not like

THE ACADEMIC.

healthy

THE WRITER.

well poppers are
i mean they're toxic chemicals you inhale
from a tiny bottle during sex
isopropyl nitrate
or nitrite or some shit
i mean it's basically doing whip-its
it's not a bowl of raw kale and a yoga class
but in moderation
eschewing
you know
long term usage
there's not really

risk of like neurological

THE ACADEMIC.

right

THE WRITER.

but we are having anal sex

i mean christ

i dare

i dare

um

someone else

i dare someone else to take that big cock of yours

THE ACADEMIC.

who

not my mother or my sister

THE WRITER.

deal

not your mother or your sister

but whomever

i dare someone else to try it

without a little help

THE ACADEMIC.

but i meant "we" as in a

a

community

THE WRITER.

community

THE ACADEMIC.

not just you and me

i meant gay

THE WRITER.

oh

homos

THE ACADEMIC.

gay men

THE WRITER.

so homos

THE ACADEMIC.

gay men

THE WRITER.

so we're a "community" now

THE ACADEMIC.

um yes we've been a community since

since stonewall certainly

harvey milk probably

ancient greece maybe

THE WRITER.

straight people use poppers

it's not like

THE ACADEMIC.

they do

THE WRITER.

of course they

so you're saying

no straight person ever in the history of

THE ACADEMIC.

that's not what i

wait what're you

THE WRITER.

gonna google popper history

THE ACADEMIC.

get back in bed

no i am serious

get back in my arms or else i'll

THE WRITER.

make me drink poppers

THE ACADEMIC.

you are a four

THE WRITER.

five

THE ACADEMIC.

year old

come here you

goddamnit i just wanna smother you

pounce and smother and

THE WRITER.

smother me

THE ACADEMIC.

murder you

THE WRITER.

after we finish talking about

i want to know your theory of

your theory on our

quote unquote

"community"

THE ACADEMIC.

ughhhhh

THE WRITER.

and its detrimental

recreational

occasional

sniffing of

THE ACADEMIC.

it's considered disgusting

it's one of the many

many things people say about gay men that

make us different

make us freaks

–

THE WRITER.

that is it

THE ACADEMIC.
what's it
THE WRITER.
this is an idiotic
THE ACADEMIC.
what
THE WRITER.
it reeks of self hatred and
THE ACADEMIC.
i am not a self hating
THE WRITER.
you are a faggot
faggots fuck in the ass
poppers feel good whilst fucking in the ass
THE ACADEMIC.
wow
when you use the word "whilst"
i get so hard
THE WRITER.
if people
THE ACADEMIC.
boing oing oing
THE WRITER.
if straight people don't like it
THE ACADEMIC.
listen
gay men had plenty of perfectly pleasurable anal sex
THE WRITER.
who have never tried it
THE ACADEMIC.
long before poppers were even
THE WRITER.
who know nothing about it

THE ACADEMIC.
in fact
i think poppers are the perfect symbol
of superfluous post-industrial hedonism and

THE WRITER.
wow
when you use the phrase
"perfectly superfluous post-industrial hedonism"
i get so hard

THE ACADEMIC.
wait I'M self hating

THE WRITER.
boing oing oing

THE ACADEMIC.
you're the one who

THE WRITER.
people whose business it isn't
judging those whose business it is
that kind of ignorance i have zero

THE ACADEMIC.
you can't even give up the word "faggot"
–

THE WRITER.
it's mine
i own it

THE ACADEMIC.
calm down and kiss

THE WRITER.
you leave me

THE ACADEMIC.
or at least massage my

THE WRITER.
no choice i

THE ACADEMIC.

i've felt it for weeks but

THE WRITER.

i am going to have to fuck your mother and sister
up their asses

THE ACADEMIC.

but i was scared

THE WRITER.

and see if they like it better
with or without

THE ACADEMIC.

to say it

THE WRITER.

poppers

(**THE WRITER** *goes to the window.*)

it's stunning out today

THE ACADEMIC.

but now i can say without fear

THE WRITER.

fuck i fucking love new york in july

THE ACADEMIC.

i mean it seemed too fast so i held back but

THE WRITER.

i mean it's humid as condoleezza's cunt but

THE ACADEMIC.

and god knows i've been

THE WRITER.

everyone wears as little as possible

THE ACADEMIC.

we've all been

THE WRITER.

you on my arm and prospect park blooming

THE ACADEMIC.
   hurt

THE WRITER.
   oh god let's get a bottle of white and

THE ACADEMIC.
   hurt before

THE WRITER.
   cook mussels and shrimp
   with corn and butter

THE ACADEMIC.
   but now i can say

THE WRITER.
   and toasted baguette

THE ACADEMIC.
   without fear

THE WRITER.
   snuggle and watch *funny girl*

THE ACADEMIC.
   that i know

THE WRITER.
   i've never seen it
   have you

THE ACADEMIC.
   i know i

THE WRITER.
   and kiss as the space between our bodies
   fills with sweat and

THE ACADEMIC.
   i love

THE WRITER.
   the stench of sex and santorum

THE ACADEMIC.
   santorum

THE WRITER.
google it
and i love

THE ACADEMIC.
but i love

THE WRITER.
new york in the summer

THE ACADEMIC.
you

The Night The Street Lights Went Dark (Part 3)
June 9, 2006

(Vivaldi plays. **THE ACADEMIC** *has in fact fallen asleep.)*

*(***THE WRITER*** *looks out the window. The street lights are still out on the block but everyone is safe. He sits in the darkness and watches* **THE ACADEMIC** *sleep. He pulls the blanket up around him.)*

Four Weeks After The Attack (Part 2)
March 15, 2011

THE WRITER.
wait
did you cut your hair again

THE ACADEMIC.
yeah

THE WRITER.
but you just went
a week ago

THE ACADEMIC.
i know i

THE WRITER.
less than a

THE ACADEMIC.
wasn't happy i

THE WRITER.
how much do they

THE ACADEMIC.
like sixty
plus tip

THE WRITER.
sixty dollars
jesus does it come with
a hand job or
a free infant or something
you spent 120 dollars in a week on two haircuts and
you

THE ACADEMIC.
it's all i can control

–

my face still looks like rocky balboa
and i have the same fucking syndrome

soldiers suffer coming back from war
what the hell do you want from

THE WRITER.

no i know
i'm sorry
i'm sorry

THE ACADEMIC.

no i know
me too
me too

–

THE WRITER.

you

THE ACADEMIC.

what

THE WRITER.

look great
your hair looks great

–

The Morning After The First Date
April 22, 2006

(**THE WRITER**, *asleep*. **THE ACADEMIC** *listens to his breathing until he stirs awake.*)

THE ACADEMIC.

morning sunshine

(**THE WRITER** *bolts upright, which hurts.*)

THE WRITER.

oh god where am

oh god

THE ACADEMIC.

no no it's fine

we're in my apartment

i brought you home

THE WRITER.

oh god oh god oh god

THE ACADEMIC.

do you remember how the night

THE WRITER.

ummm i remember the wine bar

really good conversation

a joint

puking everywhere

then maybe a staircase

with orange ish carpeting

THE ACADEMIC.

that's my hallway

park slope chic

circa '76 or so

gotta love it

THE WRITER.

you took me

THE ACADEMIC.

well i couldn't just leave you on the

THE WRITER.

oh my god

THE ACADEMIC.

tried to make you drink water but you weren't exactly

THE WRITER.

my head feels like it's filled with

THE ACADEMIC.

receptive

THE WRITER.

just poured concrete

THE ACADEMIC.

here

THE WRITER.

and angry gerbils with nunchucks

THE ACADEMIC.

drink this

THE WRITER.

thanks

i am such a

i'm so embarrassed i

what a terrible impression

who vomits on their first date

THE ACADEMIC.

three times

THE WRITER.

oh god

i am so

THE ACADEMIC.

actually it was very cute

THE WRITER.

it was anything but

THE ACADEMIC.
  you'll have to take my word
  you are
THE WRITER.
  very grateful
THE ACADEMIC.
  very charming
THE WRITER.
  to be in your bed
THE ACADEMIC.
  when puking
THE WRITER.
  and not the gutter
THE ACADEMIC.
  three times
THE WRITER.
  or dumpster
THE ACADEMIC.
  in actuality it was
THE WRITER.
  an asphalt bed
THE ACADEMIC.
  my fault
THE WRITER.
  half dead
THE ACADEMIC.
  "two more"
THE WRITER.
  i'm just not
THE ACADEMIC.
  "nightcap"
THE WRITER.
  used to mixing

THE ACADEMIC.
couldn't help it
you're

THE WRITER.
never wanna see red wine or

THE ACADEMIC.
cute and i was

THE WRITER.
mary jane ever again

THE ACADEMIC.
nervous so i

THE WRITER.
no you are cute and i was

THE ACADEMIC.
didn't pace my

THE WRITER.
nervous so i didn't pace my
–

THE ACADEMIC.
can i

THE WRITER.
you are

THE ACADEMIC.
kiss you

THE WRITER.
so sweet for

THE ACADEMIC.
now please
since we never

THE WRITER.
taking care of

THE ACADEMIC.
i know how

THE WRITER.

kissing is not a good

THE ACADEMIC.

you can repay me

THE WRITER.

idea it's

THE ACADEMIC.

i don't

THE WRITER.

my mouth tastes like

THE ACADEMIC.

care

THE WRITER.

destruction

THE ACADEMIC.

i don't

THE WRITER.

my mouth tastes like

THE ACADEMIC.

care

THE WRITER.

desolation

THE ACADEMIC.

i don't

(Mouths so close.)

The Hospital (Part 1)
February 16, 2011

> (**THE WRITER** *and* **DAN** *in a hospital waiting room. Both have iPhones out while reading* **THE ACADEMIC***'s medical chart.*)

DAN.

"of the splanchnocranium

or viscerocranium"

THE WRITER.

splanchnocranium

or viscerocranium

DAN.

let's see um

that's

oh

the face

or i mean

the front part of the skull

"splanchnocranium"

or "viscerocranium"

guess it goes by either name

so whichever one you

THE WRITER.

oh listen to this

"a mneumonic device

a mneumonic device can help medical students

memorize facial anatomy

many students favor

'virgil can not make my pet zebra laugh'

'virgil can not make my pet zebra laugh'

vomer

conchae

nasal

maxilla
mandible
palatine
zygomatic
lacrimal
'virgil can not make my pet zebra laugh'"
–

DAN.
i can't fucking believe this happened

The First Talk About Dan
June 1, 2007

THE WRITER.
    pushing the book
    and pushing the book
    and pushing the book
    but the thing about selling a book is
    you can't sell a book if nobody is buying books
    and i just don't know when the

THE ACADEMIC.
    right

THE WRITER.
    pay off comes
    maybe i should quit while i'm

THE ACADEMIC.
    oh please
    you would never
    now listen
    i picked up chicken
    so get cooking

THE WRITER.
    are you there god

THE ACADEMIC.
    and remember you don't want it to come easy

THE WRITER.
    it's me margaret

THE ACADEMIC.
    because then you'd be a spoiled little

THE WRITER.
    true but some days i think please
    please may i be a spoiled little

THE ACADEMIC.
    but all you do is complain about spoiled little

THE WRITER.
   is that all i do

   –

THE ACADEMIC.
   i plead the fifth
   but you're talented
   and a pretty good lay so

THE WRITER.
   whoa whoa whoa
   a "pretty good" lay

THE ACADEMIC.
   yeah i mean like an eight point five

THE WRITER.
   what

THE ACADEMIC.
   out of ten

THE WRITER.
   boy this day sure isn't getting any
   god is everyone in america

THE ACADEMIC.
   if i don't leave room for improvement

THE WRITER.
   everyone who makes art in america

THE ACADEMIC.
   you'll become complacent and

THE WRITER.
   fucking rich

THE ACADEMIC.
   we can't have that
   wait
   is everyone in america frank rich

THE WRITER.
   no
   fucking

THE ACADEMIC.

is everyone in america fucking frank rich

THE WRITER.

no no no

frank rich never even made an appearance in

are you even listening to

money

money

making art in america without money is just

anyway

thank you for

listening

assuming you were

christ this day

first the church

then the slug

then the letter

now i'm an eight point five

THE ACADEMIC.

wait wait wait

church

slug

letter

–

THE WRITER.

took a different walk to the train today

and passed by this this

church

called "new beginnings"

so that just made me want to kill myself

then just as i was thinking

gee i want to kill myself

that'd be a new beginning

i feel this
just this
awful
SQUISH
i look down and i'd accidentally
stepped on this
this
slug
big thing
like the size of a mouse
ripped it open in two with my sneaker
accidentally obviously
i could never
but it reminded me of
well i had this one bully
through all of elementary school
he was like a bulldog and i was a bichon frise
one day at recess
he found this slug
ran into the lunchroom
came back with salt
few grains at a time
–
i like to torture it
he said
before i kill it
–
ever since if i see a slug i i i
so then
after i murdered the slug
get a text from the roomie
letter from our landlord
raising rent 200 dollars

200 dollars

THE ACADEMIC.

that can't be legal

THE WRITER.

totally legal because we're not fucking

rent stabilized

an almost twelve percent increase

those fucking hasids

THE ACADEMIC.

whoooooa

wait

i don't think it's

THE WRITER.

no

it is these fucking hasidic jew slumlords

preaching "tikkun olam"

"heal the world" and

do unto others as

meanwhile they're the greediest money grubbing

THE ACADEMIC.

but wait a

THE WRITER.

i'd love to read the haftarah portion

about dicking people over

oh and also

i think it's because i'm gay

THE ACADEMIC.

hold on

THE WRITER.

fucking homophobic

meanwhile

jews have been discriminated against their entire

THE ACADEMIC.

wait why do you think he

did he say something to imply that he

THE WRITER.

i spend my whole life

making straight people uncomfortable

i don't need it spelled out for me

—

THE ACADEMIC.

whoa whoa whooooa do you really feel that you

wow that's a really progressive

and integrated

THE WRITER.

what

THE ACADEMIC.

i think you've internalized some really

THE WRITER.

oh come on

you think those yids are super keen on you and me
packing fudge

they don't even like it when one of their own kind

wears the wrong shade of black

i'm a faggot and a reform jew turned agnostic

and i'm not in the diamond business

i might as well be dr. mengele

oh and p.s.

they fucking smell like shit on top of it

wait

listen

i know that could sound slightly offensive but

THE ACADEMIC.

no that sounds entirely offensive but

THE WRITER.

but it is adonai's honest truth

it is like a hair salad tossed with b.o. dressing

i can't

it makes me want to
it's like i gag
it's like

THE ACADEMIC.

way to go

THE WRITER.

what

THE ACADEMIC.

way to go fighting xenophobia
with xenophobia

THE WRITER.

wait

THE ACADEMIC.

no
hey
it worked for fire

THE WRITER.

listen
live and let live but

THE ACADEMIC.

please
it's a business
new york city
a.k.a. the love of your life
he is a tough lover and he has to raise

THE WRITER.

new york is not

THE ACADEMIC.

housing taxes

THE WRITER.

a boy
new york is definitely

THE ACADEMIC.

listen to me

THE WRITER.
    a girl

THE ACADEMIC.
    they need to raise your rent
    city taxes do in fact increase
    lucky it's just 200 dollars

THE WRITER.
    just
    just 200 dollars
    i write
    for nothing
    i work
    for pennies
    they're profiteering off starving ar

THE ACADEMIC.
    the martyring of your bank account
    for the artistic betterment of society
    is not their problem
    they don't care

THE WRITER.
    they don't care
    my point exactly
    and he told my roommate
    the question isn't why the increase is so high
    but why it's taken them so long to increase it
    it's snarky

THE ACADEMIC.
    it's true

THE WRITER.
    it's vengeance
    for gentrifying their shtetl
    –
    i'm allowed that
    i'm jewish

THE ACADEMIC.
    interesting then
    you help destroy a jewish neighborhood with such glee
    –
    hey
    heeeeey
    new beginnings
    –
    after you cook this chicken
    let's go to the wine bar
THE WRITER.
    we always go to the
THE ACADEMIC.
    i know but i like the
THE WRITER.
    listen
    i came to park slope
    you haven't been to williamsburg
    to my neighborhood since
    can we just
THE ACADEMIC.
    fine
    –
THE WRITER.
    how was your
THE ACADEMIC.
    fine
    fine
THE WRITER.
    how was the
    the school thing
THE ACADEMIC.
    presentation

THE WRITER.

presentation

THE ACADEMIC.

fine

met a nice guy

works in a different department

friend of a few friends

really like him i think

THE WRITER.

oh good

you've been single too long

THE ACADEMIC.

shut up

THE WRITER.

did you get his number

did you ask him out

did he ask you out

THE ACADEMIC.

god you are such a petty

jealous

THE WRITER.

you are mine woman

THE ACADEMIC.

don't do that

i'm not a woman and you don't own me either way

i haven't even said he's gay but you just assume

you assume everyone is

your law is the "presumption of homosexuality"

it reads "gay

THE WRITER.

hey

THE ACADEMIC.

until proven straight"

THE WRITER.
>   listen
>   now and then genetics fuck up
>   and a man is born attracted to the opposite sex
>   it's really not their

THE ACADEMIC.
>   oh great

THE WRITER.
>   fault

THE ACADEMIC.
>   a genetics lesson from dr. mengele

THE WRITER.
>   we can't help

THE ACADEMIC.
>   with some gay misogyny thrown in

THE WRITER.
>   who we love

THE ACADEMIC.
>   for good measure

THE WRITER.
>   as long as they don't like
>   rub it in my face

THE ACADEMIC.
>   you'd love it if a straight guy rubbed it in your

THE WRITER.
>   and yes i am wary of the straight agenda

THE ACADEMIC.
>   right
>   what's next

THE WRITER.
>   i mean i wouldn't let a straight

THE ACADEMIC.
>   STRAIGHT MARRIAGE

THE WRITER.
watch my children

THE ACADEMIC.
of course not
could be contagious

THE WRITER.
so
is he straight
or is he normal

–

THE ACADEMIC.
he is gay

THE WRITER.
cute

THE ACADEMIC.
yes

THE WRITER.
oh yeah
would you sleep with him

THE ACADEMIC.
not again no

–

THE WRITER.
not funny

THE ACADEMIC.
oh lighten up
it's just a

THE WRITER.
not funny

THE ACADEMIC.
joke
listen othello
desdemona i.e. me

ain't gonna wind up murdered any time soon

so

(**THE ACADEMIC** *kisses* **THE WRITER**.)

THE WRITER.

is he black

THE ACADEMIC.

um

what

THE WRITER.

is he black

THE ACADEMIC.

othello

THE WRITER.

no not

of course othello was

well actually "moorish" was african

with like arab mixed in but

wait we're not talking about othello

we're talking about your new b.f.f.

THE ACADEMIC.

oh

no

but i'm confused

why do you ask if he's

THE WRITER.

it'd be hot

—

THE ACADEMIC.

you are racist

THE WRITER.

what

racist

liking black men makes me

THE ACADEMIC.
noooooo
objectifying black men makes you

THE WRITER.
no it
hmm well maybe it
no no no i think objectification is
is an honor

THE ACADEMIC.
an honor

THE WRITER.
yes
please
anyone
everyone
objectify me

THE ACADEMIC.
(now you just sound desperate)

THE WRITER.
i promise i won't

THE ACADEMIC.
next you'll be cruising craigslist

THE WRITER.
put up a fight
wait you think i've never been

THE ACADEMIC.
looking for b.b.c.

THE WRITER.
objectified myself as a

THE ACADEMIC.
as a what
gay woody allen

THE WRITER.
wait what is "b.b.c."

THE ACADEMIC.

  big black cock

  –

THE WRITER.

  now that is racist

THE ACADEMIC.

  yes

  i know

  that's why i

THE WRITER.

  so i'm racist

  but you just casually toss out

THE ACADEMIC.

  no asshole i was

  will you listen

THE WRITER.

  "b.b.c."

  holy shit

  i am literally

THE ACADEMIC.

  oh my god

  stop talking

THE WRITER.

  offended

THE ACADEMIC.

  and listen to

  wait you're OFFENDED

THE WRITER.

  i'm offended

THE ACADEMIC.

  YOU'RE offended

THE WRITER.

  i'm offended

THE ACADEMIC.
    listen
    my dear boyfriend
    sorry you had a shitty

THE WRITER.
    whoa whoa whoa
    "gay woody allen"

THE ACADEMIC.
    no
    really
    are you listening
    i am sorry your day was shit
    but where is this accusatory questioning

THE WRITER.
    DUDE you're the one who was all like
    i met a great guy
    he's swell
    and sooooo handsome
    and he might've been oppressed

THE ACADEMIC.
    oh thank god no one will ever

THE WRITER.
    and we think we might elope

THE ACADEMIC.
    hear this conversation

THE WRITER.
    i bet he's strapping

THE ACADEMIC.
    outside my kitchen

THE WRITER.
    is he strapping

THE ACADEMIC.
    sort of

THE WRITER.
> he's "sort of" strapping
> is he handsome

THE ACADEMIC.
> he is handsome

THE WRITER.
> is he tall

THE ACADEMIC.
> he's not short

THE WRITER.
> is he dark

THE ACADEMIC.
> dark
> what kind of a question is
> i mean
> he is olive complexioned
> he could be italian or
> who knows
> and honestly who cares
> i am with you
> i am with you because you look like you and i love

THE WRITER.
> right

THE ACADEMIC.
> you

THE WRITER.
> what's his handsome "sort of" strapping name

THE ACADEMIC.
> my my my
> isn't HER twat in a knot tonight

THE WRITER.
> don't do that
> i'm not a woman and it's not 1968 okay
> this isn't *boys in the band*

THE ACADEMIC.

    oh so you can call me "woman"

    but if i swap gender pronouns

    i'm setting us back four decades

    and what are YOU

    some giant throbbing phallus of hypermasculinity

    your double standards

    would make any queer studies scholar weep

    i swear you give me whiplash and

THE WRITER.

    what is his name

THE ACADEMIC.

    dan

    dan

    his name is dan

    –

    isn't that an unusually handsome and strapping name

THE WRITER.

    no

THE ACADEMIC.

    exactly

    so please

    put down the insecurity

    pick up the sauté pan and

THE WRITER.

    i don't like this quote unquote dan

THE ACADEMIC.

    make that yummy

THE WRITER.

    i smell trouble

THE ACADEMIC.

    chicken with the

THE WRITER.

    this handsome "sort of" strapping dan

who could be italian
rubs me the wrong

THE ACADEMIC.
you haven't even met

THE WRITER.
i'm a writer
i intuit
what's he do
let me guess
queer studies scholar

THE ACADEMIC.
christ
where's my hanky

THE WRITER.
what

THE ACADEMIC.
my handkerchief
my handkerchief
i'd better keep an eagle eye on it lest you

THE WRITER.
it is the green-ey'd monster
which doth mock the meat

THE ACADEMIC.
the chicken

THE WRITER.
it feeds on

THE ACADEMIC.
intuit the chicken
please intuit the chicken
just cook the goddamned chick

THE WRITER.
have you ever

THE ACADEMIC.
ever what

THE WRITER.

dated a guy who's black

–

THE ACADEMIC.

i have not

ohhh do not even begin to get all

THE WRITER.

have you slept with

THE ACADEMIC.

yes of course i've

twice

–

well

once

oh do not give me that face like

it's not like i'm opposed or

it's just never been my

THE WRITER.

thing

–

are you saying an entire race

THE ACADEMIC.

i did not say

wow you have a real way of

THE WRITER.

isn't your "thing"

THE ACADEMIC.

an uncanny ability to misconstrue

THE WRITER.

wow that's a really progressive

THE ACADEMIC.

and reconstruct

THE WRITER.

and integrated

THE ACADEMIC.
>   listen

THE WRITER.
>   i think you've internalized some really

THE ACADEMIC.
>   i will sleep with every race under the sun
>   for your interracial viewing pleasure
>   if you will just
>   reconstruct
>   the chicken

The Night After The First Fight
September 4, 2006

(An LP player plays a record.)

THE ACADEMIC.

this song on 33 1/3 sounds sooo

thank you

i love it

THE WRITER.

well i'm sorry i caused our first real fight and

THE ACADEMIC.

no i'm sorry i missed your reading but

THE WRITER.

overreacted like a drunken six

THE ACADEMIC.

if i get this good a gift

THE WRITER.

five year old who didn't

THE ACADEMIC.

every fight

THE WRITER.

get his way

THE ACADEMIC.

let's fight more often

–

i'm sorry for my comment

about your stealing

from us

THE WRITER.

thanks

and

i'm sorry for my comment about

you writing a 300 page unreadable paper

THE ACADEMIC.
    thank you

THE WRITER.
    and for my comment about
    being thankful you don't make art

THE ACADEMIC.
    thank you

THE WRITER.
    and for my comment about your being a gemini

THE ACADEMIC.
    thanks

THE WRITER.
    i didn't mean to mythologize you or
    reduce you to

THE ACADEMIC.
    i know

       (They kiss.)

The First Fight (Part 1)
September 3, 2006

THE WRITER.

which to be frank you know nothing NOTHING about
because you are in academia
so you study media
and you judge art
you may even
god forbid
critique art
but you don't make art
which to be frank
we should all probably be thankful for

THE ACADEMIC.

god you can be such a

THE WRITER.

so you don't even begin to conceive of what kind of
of blood
blood goes into

THE ACADEMIC.

you know i'm actually not a a a numbskull
"blood"
"blood"
you hyperbolize given even the tiniest

THE WRITER.

actual blood
it does take actual blood to make art
but then you don't even GET what it means
to not come
to my one time motherfucking reading

THE ACADEMIC.

you mean bloodletting
—

listen i have said i'm sorry i

THE WRITER.

so embarrassing in front of some of the most important

fucking geminis with your split personalit

never date twins

my mom always

THE ACADEMIC.

i am a human being actually

not some hocus pocus astrological

your tendency to mythologize me and reduce me to

THE WRITER.

you don't even get why not being there for me tonight

hurts

oh but good news

i bet you have a fucking theory on the matter

which you'll be eager to write some

300 page unreadable paper about

you know there is a reason theories are theories

and not fact or reality because

THEY DON'T FUCKING EXIST

THE ACADEMIC.

is this our

hey

this is our first real fight

four whole months in and this is our first real fight

—

THE WRITER.

great

do you want a fucking plaque

THE ACADEMIC.

you're drunk

THE WRITER.

so are you

here gimme your shoes

THE ACADEMIC.

 you are fucking drunk

THE WRITER.

 i'll get them bronzed

 congratulations babe

 may this fight be the first of

THE ACADEMIC.

 but you're right

THE WRITER.

 very few

THE ACADEMIC.

 i do have a theory

THE WRITER.

 now in the meantime

 put your boxing gloves back on

THE ACADEMIC.

 and i might write a 300 page paper

THE WRITER.

 "total war?"

THE ACADEMIC.

 unreadable or not

THE WRITER.

 "total!"

THE ACADEMIC.

 but at least i'm not gonna steal all this shit verbatim

 you parasite

THE WRITER.

 oh i could fucking kill

 could fucking murder

THE ACADEMIC.

 and stuff it in some bloated chapter

 of some shitty attempt at a novel

THE WRITER.

 maybe i will

THE ACADEMIC.
> are you going to make me the bad guy
>
> –

THE WRITER.
> of course not
> we're both the bad guys

The Talk About Moving In Together
August 3, 2006

THE ACADEMIC.
and you are really gonna think i'm crazy
promise not to think i'm

THE WRITER.
okay sure
what

THE ACADEMIC.
you are really gonna think i'm crazy
i don't know why
because i know it's still way way way too soon

THE WRITER.
well three months together is a long

THE ACADEMIC.
no

THE WRITER.
time

THE ACADEMIC.
it's not

THE WRITER.
well in gay months

THE ACADEMIC.
i feel like moving in with you

—

isn't that

THE WRITER.
oh

THE ACADEMIC.
nuts

THE WRITER.
kind of

THE ACADEMIC.

you promised you

THE WRITER.

kidding

i mean

i understand

we're already spending a lot of our

actually all of our

time

together

but

THE ACADEMIC.

no i know

THE WRITER.

i tried that before

and it was way too much

way too soon

individual space is necessary

THE ACADEMIC.

right

and your commitment issues would have to

THE WRITER.

my commitment issues

THE ACADEMIC.

you said the other day you have

THE WRITER.

uh

that was offhand

that was in jest

you were going on about marriage equality

i said we've got years and years before

in new york state at least

before marriage would even

would be a legal possibility
what with hernandez versus robles it's

THE ACADEMIC.

hernandez versus robles was just a setback

THE WRITER.

yeah a major setback
a recent setback
a setback directly from the new york court of appeals
a setback stating plain as day
same sex partners won't be marrying in new york state
any time

THE ACADEMIC.

a little patience

THE WRITER.

soon

THE ACADEMIC.

wouldn't kill you

THE WRITER.

anyway my comment about commitment issues was
was in jest

THE ACADEMIC.

was it

THE WRITER.

hey
can we just drop it

THE ACADEMIC.

sure
we can just drop it

THE WRITER.

yeah 'cause we're here together
and having the best time
let that be enough
for tonight

–

THE ACADEMIC.

it's more than enough

it's plenty

(They kiss.)

THE WRITER.

hey did you get a chance to read

THE ACADEMIC.

what

THE WRITER.

the short stories i sent the other

THE ACADEMIC.

oh

um

yeah

yes

one

THE WRITER.

oh neat

thanks

–

so which story did you

THE ACADEMIC.

the one about the guy and the kid and

THE WRITER.

you mean the closeted celebrity journalist

and the out gay fifteen year old who was murdered

THE ACADEMIC.

yes

THE WRITER.

oh great

so

what'd you think

THE ACADEMIC.
　　it was
　　really
　　really
　　interesting

　　–

THE WRITER.
　　you mean like actually interesting
　　or like euphemistically interesting

THE ACADEMIC.
　　actually interesting
　　you have an interesting way of
　　borrowing

THE WRITER.
　　borrowing

THE ACADEMIC.
　　from real events

THE WRITER.
　　or seeming to borrow

THE ACADEMIC.
　　seeming to borrow
　　hm
　　okay

　　–

　　would
　　would you ever write about

THE WRITER.
　　about

THE ACADEMIC.
　　events from your own
　　people from your own

THE WRITER.
　　i mean writers borrow

THE ACADEMIC.

okay

THE WRITER.

from every

where

thing

one

our experience reflects our

THE ACADEMIC.

right and would you reflect our

would you borrow

from us

THE WRITER.

not without

not with

i mean

never say never but

THE ACADEMIC.

hm

okay

–

anyway i was grateful to

for the chance to read your

THE WRITER.

okay

thanks

Four Weeks After The Attack (Part 3)
March 15, 2011

THE ACADEMIC.

oh god

my face must be all over the internet

oh god

oh god i feel

THE WRITER.

listen why don't you just stay a while longer

here

in your current apartment

THE ACADEMIC.

no no no

i just need to

i need a change of

my whole life is

THE WRITER.

or

you could

–

you are really gonna think i'm crazy

but you could

come stay with me

at my place

just for a while

just

on the couch

or

you can have my bed

i'll take the couch

–

THE ACADEMIC.

wow that's

i couldn't do that but

—

but that means a whole lot to

The Break Up On The Subway Platform
March 31, 2008

THE WRITER.
    the L
    the L train is about to
    i have to go

THE ACADEMIC.
    really

THE WRITER.
    yes

THE ACADEMIC.
    but is this really

THE WRITER.
    yes

THE ACADEMIC.
    but i don't

THE WRITER.
    i know

THE ACADEMIC.
    don't want it to

THE WRITER.
    neither do i but

THE ACADEMIC.
    but you do
    yes you do
    you do want us to end
    YOU want this
    unhappy ending
    or else you'd
    but
    but i don't
    you're the one who fucked up
    so you don't get to be the one to end it

and i have forgiven you for
i forgive you for

THE WRITER.

i am doing this for
for us
and want you to
need you to agree
say you know it's right
say this is best for

THE ACADEMIC.

no

THE WRITER.

not me
not you
but best for us
us

–

THE ACADEMIC.

no
i won't
i do not agree

THE WRITER.

well then i
i have nothing
left to say

–

i have to go

–

THE ACADEMIC.

oh god
oh god it
hurts
i want to

THE WRITER.
   it hurts me too

THE ACADEMIC.
   die

THE WRITER.
   but we're unsustainable
   it's like

THE ACADEMIC.
   it's like i'm

THE WRITER.
   the beginning of

THE ACADEMIC.
   dying

THE WRITER.
   withdrawal
   and it hurts

THE ACADEMIC.
   feels like i'm

THE WRITER.
   me too

THE ACADEMIC.
   dying
   it's like

THE WRITER.
   it makes you ill

THE ACADEMIC.
   you're killing me

THE WRITER.
   physically

THE ACADEMIC.
   killing

THE WRITER.
   sick

THE ACADEMIC.
   me
   –
   hold
THE WRITER.
   i
THE ACADEMIC.
   me

   *(***THE WRITER*** holds* **THE ACADEMIC.***)*

THE WRITER.
   okay
THE ACADEMIC.
   i love
THE WRITER.
   i know
THE ACADEMIC.
   you
   –
THE WRITER.
   the L
   the L train is
   i'm going
THE ACADEMIC.
   really
THE WRITER.
   yes
THE ACADEMIC.
   is this really
THE WRITER.
   yes
THE ACADEMIC.
   but i don't

THE WRITER.
    i know
THE ACADEMIC.
    don't want it to

The School Holiday Party
December 19, 2007

(THE ACADEMIC and DAN laughing hard, just losing their shit, like DAN just said the single funniest thing, ever. THE WRITER watches, then joins them.)

THE ACADEMIC.

oh my god you are just sooooo funny

oh thank god

my drink

and now you two can finally

dan this is my boyfriend

boyfriend this is dan

THE WRITER.

dan

hello

DAN.

hi

and merry christmas

THE WRITER.

i'm jewish

DAN.

happy chanukkah

THE WRITER.

non practicing

DAN.

oh

then happy

um

THE ACADEMIC.

new year

DAN.

new year

THE ACADEMIC.

damnit

be right back

um

you two make nice

coming

coming

(**THE ACADEMIC** *leaves.*)

DAN.

i've heard a lot about you

so nice to finally

THE WRITER.

same

the one and only dan

strapping dan

DAN.

i'm not strapping

THE WRITER.

you are sort of strapping

DAN.

though i am on a gay rowing team

THE WRITER.

no way

me too

DAN.

you are

THE WRITER.

no

honestly i didn't even know that's a thing

is that a thing

DAN.

it's a thing i do

so i hope it's a thing yeah

sorry
what do you do again

THE WRITER.

in terms of cardio

DAN.

in terms of life

THE WRITER.

oh
i write

DAN.

oh right

THE WRITER.

i am a writer

DAN.

right

THE WRITER.

and you
queer studies was it

DAN.

no i write too
by day i work here
administrate
here at the school
by night i write
fiction mainly
short stories
novellas
one novel
also a graphic novel
also poetry
long form
short form
also text collage
and experimental lit

with a post postmodern

–

basically i put weird shit on paper

THE WRITER.

you're also a

DAN.

writer yeah

oh did he never mention

THE WRITER.

no it must've magically slipped his

DAN.

well then we must know a bunch of the same

THE WRITER.

yes we might as well be one another

hi dan

i'm dan

DAN.

dan hi

would i know any of your wri

THE WRITER.

probably not

that boy

that boy and his selective

wonder what else he forgot to

DAN.

what

THE WRITER.

just funny he forgot to tell me we're both

DAN.

ah

THE WRITER.

and that you're also a member of the

you know

tribe

DAN.

    tribe

THE WRITER.

    yes

DAN.

    i'm not native american

THE WRITER.

    no i mean jewish

DAN.

    i'm not jewish

THE WRITER.

    oh

    um

    you're not

DAN.

    or

    well we don't think so

    i'm adopted so

THE WRITER.

    oh

    my mistake

DAN.

    who knows

THE WRITER.

    foot in mouth

DAN.

    could be italian

THE WRITER.

    never judge a bookwriter by its

DAN.

    could be moorish for all i

THE WRITER.

    both your ethnicity and your religion

    are none of my business to begin with

so

–

DAN.

soooooo

how about this president

THE WRITER.

pardon

DAN.

bush

THE WRITER.

oh

DAN.

he's something

THE WRITER.

yes

something

DAN.

what a mess

THE WRITER.

right

DAN.

we're in

THE WRITER.

sure are

DAN.

hopefully next election we'll

THE WRITER.

god willing

though best to leave god out of

DAN.

it's on my brain 'cause

did you read today

THE WRITER.

no i

DAN.

announced he's sending more

20,000 more troops

THE WRITER.

whoa

DAN.

21,500 actually i think

THE WRITER.

just when we most need to pull out

DAN.

exactly

THE WRITER.

it's like whose country

DAN.

i know right

THE WRITER.

do we live in

DAN.

wait i'm just remembering

i think he told me you wrote

did you write that short story that was

THE WRITER.

president bush told you about my short story

DAN.

no silly

your paramour

THE WRITER.

ahhh

DAN.

that story published in

THE WRITER.

though "paramour" refers to

an illicit lover in an adulterous

DAN.

    oh

    no

    your boyfriend told me

    you wrote that story published in

    about the closeted celebrity journalist

    and the out gay fifteen year old who was murdered

    oh man i loved that

THE WRITER.

    you read that

DAN.

    oh my god yeah it was so

    your stuff is so

THE WRITER.

    oh

    that's nice

    thank you

DAN.

    sure

    –

    hey how did you guys meet again

THE WRITER.

    oh the old fashioned way

    friendster

DAN.

    awww i remember friendster

THE WRITER.

    me too

DAN.

    except i kinda don't

THE WRITER.

    me neither

    it's all about myspace now

    so anyway we went on a friendster date

DAN.

a datester

THE WRITER.

yes it was love at first datester

so i proceeded to get wasted and throw up

DAN.

oh my god

THE WRITER.

not once

DAN.

oh no

THE WRITER.

not twice

DAN.

jesus

THE WRITER.

but no less than three times

DAN.

the postman always pukes thrice

THE WRITER.

but you know why i knew we'd

he and i would stick together

DAN.

why

THE WRITER.

i woke up in his bed

he took me home

took care of me

DAN.

aw

THE WRITER.

and then the real clincher was

we hooked up in the morning

is that too much infor

DAN.

no

THE WRITER.

yeah so

in the morning

he insisted on kissing my filthy maw and i just thought

"i'm gonna know you for a really

long

DAN.

he's the best

THE WRITER.

time"

yes he's a

DAN.

keeper

THE WRITER.

sweet man

DAN.

you two make an awfully adorable

(**THE ACADEMIC** *returns.*)

THE WRITER.

well speak of the

DAN.

were your ears

THE WRITER.

devil

DAN.

burning

THE ACADEMIC.

all good i hope

what were you two

THE WRITER.

never hurts to

THE ACADEMIC.
>talking about

THE WRITER.
>hope

DAN.
>vomit

THE ACADEMIC.
>perfect
>
>–

THE WRITER.
>and so what about you

DAN.
>me

THE WRITER.
>where's your boyfriend

DAN.
>um
>gosh
>i don't know
>but if you find out he exists
>please tell him i'm waiting
>green light means go
>heart for sale
>actually
>i should
>will you guys be here for
>i'll catch up with you in a

THE WRITER.
>don't

DAN.
>sec

THE WRITER.
>dawdle

>>(**DAN** *leaves.*)

THE ACADEMIC.
unbelievable
green-ey'd monster one minute
"soooo where's your boyfriend"
flirt the next

THE WRITER.
i am not a

THE ACADEMIC.
you are THE flirt
and hey it worked on me
but still
there are signs on every highway
tunnel
bridge
in the tri-state area
directing traffic and single men
to brooklyn
for a taste

THE WRITER.
you know i don't fuck truckers

THE ACADEMIC.
and you know

THE WRITER.
anymore

THE ACADEMIC.
i don't even mind
because i trust you

THE WRITER.
you are so inside your head
it's like you're outside

THE ACADEMIC.
i trust our relationship
i trust our

THE WRITER.
or up your own

THE ACADEMIC.
    love
THE WRITER.
    ass

    —
THE ACADEMIC.
    you attracted to him

    —
THE WRITER.
    yes
THE ACADEMIC.
    good
    then i have permission to get enraged at you
    like you got at me
THE WRITER.
    just because i think he's attractive
    doesn't mean
THE ACADEMIC.
    precisely
THE WRITER.
    this whole conversation
    makes me feel like
THE ACADEMIC.
    a hypocrite
THE WRITER.
    i am not a flirt
THE ACADEMIC.
    are you fucking kidding me
    are you seriously fucking kidding me
    your name is flirt
    you embody
    you encapsulate flirt
    your atoms aren't carbon
    they are flit and flaunt

flatter and giggle
wink and nudge
dropped pencil
accidental touch
you taught cupid
you
are
flirt

The Night The Street Lights Went Dark: Part 4
June 9, 2006

(**THE WRITER** *and* **THE ACADEMIC** *simultaneously explode in orgasms.*)

THE WRITER.

that was

THE ACADEMIC.

yeah

THE WRITER.

so

THE ACADEMIC.

i know

THE WRITER.

you're

THE ACADEMIC.

you too

THE WRITER.

my god i

THE ACADEMIC.

i know

THE WRITER.

it's

THE ACADEMIC.

right

THE WRITER.

really

THE ACADEMIC.

i

THE WRITER.

just

THE ACADEMIC.

man

THE WRITER.

you

THE ACADEMIC.

i

THE WRITER.

you

THE ACADEMIC.

you

THE WRITER.

i

THE ACADEMIC.

love

THE WRITER.

what

THE ACADEMIC.

i love

THE WRITER.

oh

THE ACADEMIC.

you

THE WRITER.

you

THE ACADEMIC.

i love you

THE WRITER.

love

THE ACADEMIC.

yeah

THE WRITER.

me

—

THE ACADEMIC.

whoa

THE WRITER.
right
we

THE ACADEMIC.
yeah

THE WRITER.
we're there

THE ACADEMIC.
we are

THE WRITER.
already

THE ACADEMIC.
too soon

THE WRITER.
don't know
don't think so
i mean i
do too

(They kiss.)

THE ACADEMIC.
it's like you're listening
i can tell you listen to me and
i'm
i'm

THE WRITER.
what

THE ACADEMIC.
happy
you make me happy

THE WRITER.
you make me happy too

(They kiss.)

THE ACADEMIC.

do you

THE WRITER.

what

THE ACADEMIC.

think it's bad

THE WRITER.

what

THE ACADEMIC.

that we use poppers

The Hospital (Part 2)
February 16, 2011

(The hospital waiting room. DAN *emerges from the recovery room, not looking good.)*

DAN.

you can

—

—

he's

—

—

*(*DAN *nods.* THE WRITER *starts to go into the recovery room but* DAN *stops him.)*

just

don't cry

The Second Talk About Monogamy
January 2, 2008

THE ACADEMIC.
myspace friends with dan

THE WRITER.
huh
who

THE ACADEMIC.
i see you became myspace friends with dan
dan
you met like two weeks ago
at the school holiday party

THE WRITER.
ohhh strapping dan
yeah

THE ACADEMIC.
did he friend you or did you friend him

THE WRITER.
is nothing sacred

THE ACADEMIC.
uh huh
next you two will be picking out china

THE WRITER.
oh please
you're the one who hung on his every word like
wait c'mere

THE ACADEMIC.
can we have sex

THE WRITER.
no no no
you gotta watch this video

THE ACADEMIC.
is it porn

THE WRITER.

no it's this high school graduation

THE ACADEMIC.

the least sexy sentence you could've possibly

THE WRITER.

and there's this like sixteen year old kid

getting an award for

being brilliant or whatever

and in the middle of his acceptance speech

the kid like full on announces he's gay

to his entire high school and all these parents

i mean like he prepared a written

THE ACADEMIC.

kind of literalizes the phrase "acceptance speech"

THE WRITER.

right and the fact that it was recorded

that it spread all over the internet within a few days

recorded by his parents no less

in pride of their son's bravery and

THE ACADEMIC.

it's incredibly public

that's for sure

–

THE WRITER.

i thought you of all people

THE ACADEMIC.

me

THE WRITER.

would appreciate

THE ACADEMIC.

what

THE WRITER.

the use of the medium

the use of the internet for good

THE ACADEMIC.

sure

he's brave

THE WRITER.

uh yeah he is

to be true to himself

this kid risks having the shit beaten out of him

every day

you don't find the documentation

of such radical change

THE ACADEMIC.

sure

THE WRITER.

pertinent to how media not only records

but can actually affect

like

social change

THE ACADEMIC.

well you think everyone should

THE WRITER.

what

THE ACADEMIC.

you see coming out of the closet

in astonishingly black and white

THE WRITER.

huh

THE ACADEMIC.

absolutes

THE WRITER.

what do you

THE ACADEMIC.

like that story you wrote

about the closeted celebrity and the out fifteen year old

THE WRITER.

the out gay fifteen year old who got murdered

THE ACADEMIC.

right

THE WRITER.

who got shot twice in the back of his head
in his high school computer lab

THE ACADEMIC.

right

THE WRITER.

which is based on a true
which is based on actual events in califor

THE ACADEMIC.

yes but in the story you juxtapose that murder
with this closeted celebrity journalist "character"
reporting on the murder
drawing a parallel that

THE WRITER.

illuminates

THE ACADEMIC.

emotionally manipulates your reader into feeling
i mean you basically blame some celebrity in new york
not being out
for the ignorance of some random homophobe in
california committing a

THE WRITER.

indirectly
but yes
i do

THE ACADEMIC.

random crime
it's

THE WRITER.

"random"

THE ACADEMIC.

contrived

THE WRITER.

are you kidding me "random"

being shot for being gay is not random

THE ACADEMIC.

and then

through your thinly veiled

closeted celebrity journalist "character"

you effectively OUT

that real life closeted celebrity journalist

god you're like the perez hilton of fiction writing

–

THE WRITER.

um

wow

are you literally arguing with me about a story i wrote

that draws a correlation

between the murder of a gay kid

and a closeted celebrity

a closeted celebrity JOURNALIST

who allegedly reports with 360 degrees

of truthfulness and transparency

but can't say "i'm gay" out loud in public

you

who like the majority of liberal americans

seem to think we're living in some

"post gay" fantasia

where kids aren't being beaten for being

where kids aren't being KILLED for being gay

are you literally arguing with me

that coming out is a personal choice

because of course it's a personal choice
but it's also a political choice
it is a political choice to say "i'm gay"
and that goes tenfold if you're famous
are you literally

THE ACADEMIC.

i'm not saying a gay celebrity journalist
shouldn't come out
i'm just saying on an individual level
not everything is so simple for every

–

will you stop watching that clip on repeat
and engage in conversation with

THE WRITER.

i can't help it
the boy is cute

–

THE ACADEMIC.

the boy is like sixteen

THE WRITER.

hey if there's grass on the field
play ball

THE ACADEMIC.

that's disgusting

THE WRITER.

no
that's a joke

THE ACADEMIC.

yeah perpetuating the "joke" of gay men
as predators and pedophiles

THE WRITER.

jesus christ

THE ACADEMIC.

is hilarious

THE WRITER.

you're just jealous

here i'll message the kid

and see if he's into a threesome

–

THE ACADEMIC.

you're just dying aren't you

THE WRITER.

dying to have sex with that sixteen year old

no

THE ACADEMIC.

no

to have sex with me and

someone else

at least admit you're

THE WRITER.

listen let's just drop the whole

THE ACADEMIC.

oh of course

"let's just drop it"

fucking obnoxious way of killing communica

THE WRITER.

forgot i'm dating such a goddamned bastion of romantic
communication

THE ACADEMIC.

excuse me

THE WRITER.

you know babe

sometimes i'm feeling something

and i say "i'm feeling this"

and then you're like

–

and then i'm like "and i'm also feeling this"

and then you're like

—

and then i'm like "sooooo how do YOU feel"
and from the look on your face you'd think i asked
"hey can i wax your chest and then dip your balls in
acid"
no
honestly
i am humbled
being accused of closing off
by a boy who cannot say "i feel angry" or
by a boyfriend who can't discuss any significant feelings
at all
without a stop to the liquor store
WAIT where are you

     (**THE ACADEMIC** *leaves the room.*)

—

—

—

oh so when you want to go you go
but if i say "let's drop it"
it's hiroshima

—

—

—

fucking child
hypocritical fucking

     (**THE WRITER** *leaves the room too.*)

—

—

—

     (**THE ACADEMIC** *returns, after what should feel
     like a little too long.*)

—

are you back yet

THE ACADEMIC.

i'm here

> *(***THE WRITER** *returns too. Silence for a moment.)*

pedophilia jokes aside i will try to make more of a

to make a better effort to

i am trying

to be here and talk

to tell you what is going on

inside me

–

THE WRITER.

thank you

–

THE ACADEMIC.

i get

i feel jealous when

–

you want to have a threesome and it makes me feel
jealous

THE WRITER.

i don't want to have

THE ACADEMIC.

jesus will you let me talk

i can't projectile vomit my emotions like you okay

it's

vulnerable

for me

and i need

–

THE WRITER.

sorry

THE ACADEMIC.

thank you

it makes me feel like i am not enough

like you are not happy

or pleased

THE WRITER.

okay

–

THE ACADEMIC.

is that all you have to say

THE WRITER.

i didn't know i was allowed to

THE ACADEMIC.

oh my god you are such

THE WRITER.

talk now

THE ACADEMIC.

a fucking brat

i think growing up watching your parents' disastrous

THE WRITER.

yeah i know

THE ACADEMIC.

means you equate combat

THE WRITER.

yes i know

THE ACADEMIC.

with love

THE WRITER.

yes

thanks

i have been in therapy for fucking years because of

but that is unrelated to

THE ACADEMIC.

is it

i think maybe it's related to everything

–

THE WRITER.

i am happy in bed with you

like extremely happy

i

perhaps

do possess a

a

THE ACADEMIC.

a what

THE WRITER.

an adventurous streak

which

perhaps

perhaps you don't

–

THE ACADEMIC.

am i boring

THE WRITER.

no

not at all

but i have an overactive imagination

i get off on fantasy

and that is a part of me you must embrace

so for me it's recreation to say

"if we did have a threesome

who would it be with"

it's like

"if we did buy a mediterranean island

which would it be"

–

THE ACADEMIC.

you watch too much porn

THE WRITER.

i barely watch porn

well maybe but
wait what are you
okay
okay
we have to get to the seed of the problem
or else this is like pulling up weeds without the root and

THE ACADEMIC.

and what is the seed

THE WRITER.

the seed is not porn
the seed is this oddly
forgive me
puritanical notion that
a threesome is wrong
or dangerous
or dirty
that there is one way
one right way
to love and be loved
to express sexuality

THE ACADEMIC.

i'm listening
had no idea i'm in a relationship with anna madrigal
so bear with me while i adjust to this *tales of the city* life
but

THE WRITER.

well yes i do hold an admittedly maupin point of view

THE ACADEMIC.

well remember the bathhouses did lead to

THE WRITER.

hey
may those bathhouses rest in peace
we made it through ed fucking koch

THE ACADEMIC.

well some did

THE WRITER.

that fucking faggot

only to get giuliani's war on sex

rest in peace to free love and sexual liberation and

THE ACADEMIC.

rest in peace also to the

what

half million men who were dead or dying by 1986 or
198

THE WRITER.

wait are you saying the bathhouses caused a.i.d.s.

because in reality it's a little more compli

THE ACADEMIC.

no but

THE WRITER.

i think your overall take on monogamy is a little

THE ACADEMIC.

what

THE WRITER.

reaganized

THE ACADEMIC.

i will kill you

THE WRITER.

i mean

post eighties we were certainly all brought up

THE ACADEMIC.

educated

THE WRITER.

cautious

THE ACADEMIC.

aware

THE WRITER.

scared

THE ACADEMIC.

babe i don't think a threesome will give me h.i.v.

i think a threesome
will confuse our entire rule system and
oh and by the way
i think it's reprehensible when you call ed koch a

THE WRITER.

what
a faggot
but he IS a faggot
ed koch is a big fucking faggot
a nelly cocksucking cum guzzling faggot
who will never come out as such
and who let thousands of his brothers and sisters die

THE ACADEMIC.

wow
you really think

THE WRITER.

miserable deaths instead of

THE ACADEMIC.

that you're larry kramer

THE WRITER.

throwing them a lifesaver

THE ACADEMIC.

but you are no larry kramer

THE WRITER.

from the safety of his big fat political yacht
the sixteen year old boy in that video
that sixteen year old who came out
in front of his entire school
that sixteen year old has a hell of a lot of men to thank
most of whom are six fucking feet under
and not one of them is ed koch

THE ACADEMIC.

okay fine i won't thank ed koch
for all the sixteen year olds you can now fuck

THE WRITER.

you are completely mangling my entire

gay men as a as a as a

THE ACADEMIC.

community

THE WRITER.

fine a COMMUNITY

have fought not just for acceptance

but for freedom

to be who we are

THE ACADEMIC.

you mean to fuck who we want

THE WRITER.

YES

THE ACADEMIC.

BUT I JUST WANT TO HAVE SEX WITH YOU

just you

can you understand that

look forward

look at what we've won

and appreciate that we can do this

i want you

just

you

–

–

THE WRITER.

okay

okay and

for now i can handle that

–

THE ACADEMIC.

dan

THE WRITER.

what

THE ACADEMIC.

for me it would be dan

THE WRITER.

handsome

"sort of" strapping

could be italian

THE ACADEMIC.

dan

yes

if we brought someone in to

to share

like a

a

THE WRITER.

sweater

plate of ribs

anecdote

THE ACADEMIC.

yeah for me it would be dan

but

it's not going to happen

or at least

not soon

THE WRITER.

okay

but just

THE ACADEMIC.

what

THE WRITER.

remember your dictum

THE ACADEMIC.

my dictum

THE WRITER.

you said never

say never

–

THE ACADEMIC.

can we have sex now

THE WRITER.

yes please

THE ACADEMIC.

like right now

THE WRITER.

oh yeah

THE ACADEMIC.

thank you

and thank you for being patient

and talking this out with me

THE WRITER.

you are very

THE ACADEMIC.

your feelings are

THE WRITER.

welcome

THE ACADEMIC.

legitimate

even if i feel completely

After The Marriage Equality Rally
February 17, 2008

(**THE WRITER** *takes leave of a party happening in the other room. Out of sight,* **THE ACADEMIC** *drunkenly chants:*)

THE ACADEMIC.

what do we want
MARRIAGE EQUALITY
when do we want it
NOW
what do we want
MARRIAGE EQUALITY

(**THE ACADEMIC** *enters.*)

babe come back to the
everyone is
you said you wanted to try the

THE WRITER.

i'm not sure anymore

–

it's cocaine
it's addictive

THE ACADEMIC.

it's natural
it's made from plants
GAY STRAIGHT BLACK WHITE
MARRIAGE IS A CIVIL RIGHT
whoa
making social strides gets me horny
babe we're celebrating fighting the good fight
a little setback sure but hey we're getting closer
eliot spitzer man
spitzer's got our back

THE WRITER.

i'm not sure about that either

THE ACADEMIC.

that spitzer's got our back

trust me dude

he does

THE WRITER.

no

marriage equality

THE ACADEMIC.

um

so you're advocating for marriage INequality

THE WRITER.

no but

i'm proud to be

to be part of a community

that's resisted traditional notions of marriage and

THE ACADEMIC.

oh suddenly you consider yourself part of the community

THE WRITER.

that's called marriage out

on being an old ass bullshit way of controlling people and

THE ACADEMIC.

oh just shoot me in the face right now

listen

don't debate

just let loose

you're a social person already

a little coke will just be a boost

THE WRITER.

like coffee

THE ACADEMIC.

exactly like coffee

notably strong coffee

THE WRITER.

listen i want to but i just don't think tonight is

> (**DAN** *comes crashing in with a protest sign: "I'm here to meet my HUSBAND!"*)

DAN.

hey where did you two limp wristed lovebirds disappear to

oh

am i interrupting for real

THE ACADEMIC.

no no not at all

DAN.

party's no fun without its hosts

THE ACADEMIC.

we'll be right

no wait

actually

stay with us for a sec

trying to convince stubborn stacey here

to lighten up and have a little

THE WRITER.

he's trying to use junior high level peer pressure to

THE ACADEMIC.

have fun

THE WRITER.

destroy my nasal passages and cerebral cortex

DAN.

oh

the blow i got

yeah you should totally join us

it's made from plants

see you guys in a sec

WHO CARES WHAT CHENEY SAYS

HIS DAUGHTER'S STILL A LEZ

(**DAN** *leaves.* **THE ACADEMIC** *slaps his ass as he does.*)

THE WRITER.

why is he

THE ACADEMIC.

what

THE WRITER.

here

THE ACADEMIC.

we are friends

–

listen

i don't mean to

unfairly put pressure on

THE WRITER.

thanks

–

THE ACADEMIC.

but is it cool if i do a little more

THE WRITER.

um

THE ACADEMIC.

listen we're all having a good

THE WRITER.

but then you're going to get all

THE ACADEMIC.

time

THE WRITER.

coke crazed and i'll be

THE ACADEMIC.

babe control your

well destiny sounds ridiculous

but at least control your night

listen it's not my fault you come from a long line

of alcoholics and compulsive gamblers
but you are you
not them
–

THE WRITER.

you're right
i can only control my own actions
i can't control yours
god knows

THE ACADEMIC.

well then
see ya later

THE WRITER.

even if you are half of a pair

THE ACADEMIC.

i'm off on my coke crazed coke binge

(**THE ACADEMIC** *exits.*)

THE WRITER.

as if us getting married would be a good

The Night With Dan
February 25, 2008

(**THE WRITER** *and* **DAN** *and the LP player. Beers.*
Light, barely.)

DAN.

this song on 33 1/3 sounds sooo

THE WRITER.

i know

i gave him the record player

(**THE WRITER** *touches* **DAN.**)

DAN.

so

when is he

THE WRITER.

what

DAN.

coming home

THE WRITER.

home

uh

he's

sorry i thought you knew

DAN.

knew

THE WRITER.

he's not

DAN.

he's not

THE WRITER.

he's out of town

DAN.

oh

THE WRITER.
    visiting friends

DAN.
    oh
    i assumed
    when you
    you said come over to our

THE WRITER.
    i meant his
    i'm staying here mostly while he's

DAN.
    oh but i
    i assumed
    sorry
    um
    should i go
    i should go

THE WRITER.
    no no no

DAN.
    no

THE WRITER.
    no

DAN.
    i thought the three of us would

        (**THE WRITER** *takes* **DAN***'s hand and places it on his chest.*)

    is this

        (**THE WRITER** *kisses* **DAN**.)

Two And A Half Years After The Break Up
September 14, 2010

*(***THE WRITER*** and* ***THE ACADEMIC*** *run into one other.)*

THE ACADEMIC.

so crazy

THE WRITER.

oh my god

THE ACADEMIC.

to run into you here

(They negotiate a hug.)

THE WRITER.

yeah i mean what are the chances

we haven't really

we haven't exactly

THE ACADEMIC.

we haven't seen each other for two and a half years

THE WRITER.

no no no it's only been

oh

yeah

two and a half years

well you look

amazing

THE ACADEMIC.

oh

thanks

you look great

THE WRITER.

thanks

THE ACADEMIC.

too

THE WRITER.

i did have some work done

THE ACADEMIC.

oh yeah

THE WRITER.

well just my nose

THE ACADEMIC.

ah

THE WRITER.

and cheeks

chin

eyes

teeth

lypo

THE ACADEMIC.

lypo

THE WRITER.

i have a wonderful team of surgeons

but there is a LOT of skin

pulled back behind my ears you'll never see

THE ACADEMIC.

zing

THE WRITER.

buh dum bum

THE ACADEMIC.

oh boy

still cute when you make onomatopoeic

THE WRITER.

what

no

THE ACADEMIC.

sounds

—

THE WRITER.

sooooo life's been good the past two

THE ACADEMIC.

two and a half

THE WRITER.

years

THE ACADEMIC.

yes and no

things have been

intense

THE WRITER.

i see

or don't see

–

but i'm listening

THE ACADEMIC.

well

dan and i

THE WRITER.

yes

how are you and dan

THE ACADEMIC.

well we

THE WRITER.

but before you answer

have we ever acknowledged

THE ACADEMIC.

no

THE WRITER.

how ironic

THE ACADEMIC.

but let me guess

you wish to acknowledge it now

THE WRITER.
    i do
    that after we separated

THE ACADEMIC.
    yes

THE WRITER.
    and after what transpired
    between me and dan

THE ACADEMIC.
    yes

THE WRITER.
    you two
    you and dan

THE ACADEMIC.
    right

THE WRITER.
    dan and you

THE ACADEMIC.
    right

THE WRITER.
    are together

THE ACADEMIC.
    actually we got engaged
    –

THE WRITER.
    en
    engaged
    wow i
    i had no i
    that's
    congratula
    but
    wait it's not even
    it's still not legal yet in new york state so

THE ACADEMIC.

i moved

there are actually forty-nine other states

but anyway

then we broke off the engagement

THE WRITER.

oh

THE ACADEMIC.

and broke up

THE WRITER.

oh no

THE ACADEMIC.

last week

THE WRITER.

oh god i'm so sorry i

THE ACADEMIC.

yeah so i just got back to the city and

THE WRITER.

i am so sorry

i had no idea that you

we haven't exactly spoken since

THE ACADEMIC.

yes well

remember how

at the end

THE WRITER.

yes

THE ACADEMIC.

you completely trampled my

THE WRITER.

oh

THE ACADEMIC.

heart

left me ruined for a

THE WRITER.
ah

THE ACADEMIC.
time
even though i forgave you
you still ended it not long after
actually if memory serves
i sobbed on a subway platform and you got on the train
even though i forgave you for what you did
you still ended it
and that required
some distance
some healing
some
time
–

THE WRITER.
i am sorry

THE ACADEMIC.
yeah

THE WRITER.
no
listen to me
i am sorry for ruining everything we
and never apologizing

THE ACADEMIC.
thank you
but you did apologize
you apologized a hundred times

THE WRITER.
but it's taken me two and a half years to actually mean it

After The Night With Dan
February 28, 2008

THE WRITER.

i can only apologize so many

–

i need to know if

if this means

if this is a hurdle we can't

if this one instance of infidelity

forever alters your trust in me

in our ongoing relationship

or

is it something that ends

the relationship

ends

we end

THE ACADEMIC.

you know the worst is i never saw it coming

how capable you'd be of

and with the friend you repeatedly and relentlessly

insinuated I'D be likely to

not to mention the friend i

i told you i'd consider joining us in our

–

and yeah

you would like it to be that easy

for me to say this is over

you're off the hook

you'll miss me but then

being single wouldn't be so bad

well fuck you

i'm your boyfriend

which means i love you

which means we have a commitment
no contract
certainly not yet
but still a commitment
which means i'm staying by your side
even as you make idiotic fucking mistakes
–
now
we have a lot of work to do
onward ho

The Hospital (Part 3)
February 16, 2011

(The hospital waiting room.)

THE WRITER.

can i see

> (**THE WRITER** *moves to* **DAN** *to share the medical chart.*)

jesus

crushed

DAN.

vomer

inferior nasal concha

middle nasal concha

anterior nasal spine and

perpendicular plate

also pulver

THE WRITER.

pulverized

temporal process

zygomatic process

infraorbital foramen and

zygomaticofacial foramen

frac

DAN.

fractured

as well as

orbital surface and

orbital plates

shat

THE WRITER.

shattered

shattered ramus

alveolar crest

temporal and

DAN.

ethmoid bone

misaligned

–

jesus is there anything they didn't

THE WRITER.

yes

wait

his ears

(the auricle

DAN.

auricle and

tympanic membrane

THE WRITER.

the malleus

the incus

the stapes)

they're all intact

–

his hearing

DAN.

his hearing is fine

The Dinner Before The Attack
February 15, 2011

THE WRITER.
a toast
to the um
audaciously hopeful
commitment to our friendship

THE ACADEMIC.
yes to
new beginnings
–
the last time i saw you
we ran into each other at
that was right after dan and i
called off the engagement

THE WRITER.
yes
i remember

THE ACADEMIC.
i thought on facebook
there'd be a relationship status for that but no
anyway

THE WRITER.
anyway
i miss you
i am very glad we're committing to a friendship

THE ACADEMIC.
so am i

THE WRITER.
good
so
you said you're back in school

THE ACADEMIC.
>getting my phd actually
>in media's effect on queer culture

THE WRITER.
>wow
>i think that's great

THE ACADEMIC.
>do you

THE WRITER.
>i really do
>that's important
>that's groundbreaking

THE ACADEMIC.
>thank you
>and how is writing

THE WRITER.
>oh you know
>it's coming

THE ACADEMIC.
>rumor is

THE WRITER.
>along

THE ACADEMIC.
>coming well
>i heard you sold something

THE WRITER.
>i sold something

THE ACADEMIC.
>congratulations
>no i mean it
>you're brave and

THE WRITER.
>what

THE ACADEMIC.

i'm really proud of you

THE WRITER.

thank you

–

and now you're living

THE ACADEMIC.

yup

here

your hood

williamsburg

THE WRITER.

that is so

THE ACADEMIC.

what

THE WRITER.

ironic

THE ACADEMIC.

yes

williamsburg is an entire territory

founded on the conviction of irony

THE WRITER.

because back when we were

THE ACADEMIC.

i know

THE WRITER.

you remember you were resistant to coming here at all

THE ACADEMIC.

i know

THE WRITER.

i practically lived in your apartment

THE ACADEMIC.

i know

THE WRITER.

    i practically lived in park slope

    but i think by the end i made it very clear

    the privileged parents of park slope

    and their illusion of diversity

    juxtaposed with

    well let's face it

    basically full out racial segregation

    wasn't exactly suiting my

THE ACADEMIC.

    oh lord if this isn't the pot smoking pot

    calling the kettle

    first of all darling

    people with privilege

    shouldn't be allowed to talk about privilege

    they're already allowed to do everything else

    second of all

    don't talk to me about racial segregation in park slope

    because guess what

    every single one of williamsburg's endemic minorities

    have been pushed to its fringes by

THE WRITER.

    park slope isn't fun

THE ACADEMIC.

    middle to upper class white kids

THE WRITER.

    park slope lacks community

THE ACADEMIC.

    and i can't with you and "community"

    if there's a lack of it you complain

    if there's a bounty of it you complain

    and yeah

    wow

    what a melting pot williamsburg is

THE WRITER.
   at least it ain't boring

THE ACADEMIC.
   a five million dollar trustfundee
   living in the same shitty new highrise condo
   as a fifteen million dollar trustfundee
   does not a melting pot

THE WRITER.
   oh please
   with bloomberg serving a third term
   the whole city is a playground for the wealthy
   it's not just williamsburg
   or park slope
   listen
   the point is
   you've come around
   you're here now
   and i dare say
   you like it
   –

THE ACADEMIC.
   listen
   when we met
   i was uber nesting
   i needed to be home
   i was depressed

THE WRITER.
   wow
   while we were

THE ACADEMIC.
   this wasn't

THE WRITER.
   the whole time we

THE ACADEMIC.

secret information

remember i did start therapy

and anti anxiety meds

and i also think

THE WRITER.

what

THE ACADEMIC.

we weren't always

THE WRITER.

what

THE ACADEMIC.

happy

THE WRITER.

right but what relationship is always hap

THE ACADEMIC.

but i think it made me drink more

—

THE WRITER.

i'm sorry

are you blaming me for

THE ACADEMIC.

no

of course not

what i'm saying is

i am sorry

i felt a need to be in my own home

i did not accommodate yours

i refused to compromise

THE WRITER.

usually that's something i admire

i'm sorry i didn't then

—

THE ACADEMIC.
   well
   now it's water under the
THE WRITER.
   long ago
THE ACADEMIC.
   far away
   let's skip to today
THE WRITER.
   yes
   today
THE ACADEMIC.
   so did you hear
THE WRITER.
   what
THE ACADEMIC.
   today
THE WRITER.
   what
THE ACADEMIC.
   d.o.m.a.
THE WRITER.
   the west village coffee shop
   shit did it burn down or
THE ACADEMIC.
   no asshole
   the defense of marriage act
THE WRITER.
   ah
   clinton's "defense of marriage act"
THE ACADEMIC.
   yes but obama today

THE WRITER.
 motherfucking clinton

THE ACADEMIC.
 internfucking clinton
 but just today obama

THE WRITER.
 obama
 yes i saw

THE ACADEMIC.
 he declared d.o.m.a.
 unconstitutional
 it's historic
 burn that homophobic shit down to the

THE WRITER.
 step in the right

THE ACADEMIC.
 i mean it's taking a little

THE WRITER.
 direction

THE ACADEMIC.
 time but

THE WRITER.
 but he sure is taking his

THE ACADEMIC.
 but at least he's finally

THE WRITER.
 time
 and didn't he only address section 3

THE ACADEMIC.
 actually doing something

THE WRITER.
 which defines marriage as a heterosexual

THE ACADEMIC.
 not talking

but doing

THE WRITER.

sorry i mean between a man and a

THE ACADEMIC.

following through on his

THE WRITER.

not man

THE ACADEMIC.

woman

they're called women

THE WRITER.

section 2 of the defense of marriage act

on the other hand

THE ACADEMIC.

gay misogyny is hilarious

THE WRITER.

section 2 requires one state to

THE ACADEMIC.

change

THE WRITER.

to recognize marriages from another state

THE ACADEMIC.

change we can believe in

THE WRITER.

but he didn't address section 2 did he

THE ACADEMIC.

sure it's taking him a little longer than

THE WRITER.

and either way i think the whole process

legislatively still has a long time to

and he

obama

keeps fucking folding and stretching

doubling back and

THE ACADEMIC.
    i think it's momentous
    i am proud today
    i am actually proud
    to be

THE WRITER.
    please don't say "an american"

THE ACADEMIC.
    an american
    another round
    let's get another round
    and drink to progress

THE WRITER.
    time will tell

THE ACADEMIC.
    forward motion

THE WRITER.
    i guess

THE ACADEMIC.
    evolution

THE WRITER.
    we shall see

THE ACADEMIC.
    human beings can change
    people can

THE WRITER.
    time will

THE ACADEMIC.
    change

THE WRITER.
    tell

THE ACADEMIC.
    just when you think they can't
    people can actually

The Lush Soap Store (Part 2)
February 16, 2011

LAILA.

hi

THE WRITER.

hi

LAILA.

how's it going

THE WRITER.

it

it goes okay

how're you

LAILA.

i'm great

i'm laila

i'll be your bath specialist today

do you need help with anything

THE WRITER.

um

for now

just looking

LAILA.

for anything in particular

THE WRITER.

um

i'm not sure

just going to

look around and

LAILA.

sure sure sure

take your time and

THE WRITER.

thanks

LAILA.

if you need anything

THE WRITER.

thank you

LAILA.

just ask

THE WRITER.

i will

—

LAILA.

have you tried our bath bombs

THE WRITER.

no

LAILA.

they're amaaazing

THE WRITER.

they sound

um

violent

LAILA.

ha

no silly

THE WRITER.

do they um

explode

LAILA.

no

well

i guess sort of

an explosion of happiness

THE WRITER.

now that is a grand claim

LAILA.

(they make us say that

don't tell my manager i told you)

THE WRITER.

(i won't)

LAILA.

but they do explode with glitter

and this one with salts and perfumes

and this one with real dried lavender

THE WRITER.

neat

water's the detonator

LAILA.

the detonator

THE WRITER.

when you drop the bath bomb in the water

LAILA.

ohhhhh

yes of course

water's the detonator

so

is it for a special occasion

or for anyone in particular

orrrr

THE WRITER.

what

LAILA.

for that special someone

THE WRITER.

um

well

wow

this sounds dramatic

LAILA.

i love drama

THE WRITER.

but my um

my friend um

my ex boyfriend actually

LAILA.

oh

THE WRITER.

was um

attacked

um

LAILA.

oh

THE WRITER.

last night

and

uh

LAILA.

oh my god

THE WRITER.

yeah

one minute you're

having dinner together

discussing obama

homophobic laws being repealed

and how far we've

then you hug good bye

say "see you soon"

on his way home some teenagers make a comment

ask him if he's a boy or a girl and

and it was

LAILA.

oh god

THE WRITER.

a hate crime so

LAILA.

oh my god

THE WRITER.

pretty bad so

he's in the hospital

and

is in the middle of a really big

seven hour long

surgery today

a team of surgeons are

as we speak actually

and so i

a major

facial reconstruction so

metal plates permanently implanted in his

so i'm going to visit after work because

i mean i don't even know if he'll

be conscious again yet but

i thought some soaps

and facial

god i don't know

moisturizers

creams

LAILA.

bath bombs

THE WRITER.

yes some bath bombs

might make

might help

him feel

feel

oh god

i'm sorry

i haven't really had a chance to

LAILA.

oh god don't worry

THE WRITER.

say any of this

LAILA.

it's okay

THE WRITER.

out loud

oh god

i'm crying

in the lush bath soap store

LAILA.

it's

THE WRITER.

no offense

LAILA.

are you kidding

i fucking hate it here

THE WRITER.

i'm at work all day

with it sitting

here in my chest

going about things like it's

LAILA.

where did it

THE WRITER.

in brooklyn

LAILA.

oh my god

THE WRITER.
in williamsburg
in brooklyn
in my own

LAILA.
oh here
tissue

THE WRITER.
and you just think

LAILA.
why is this still happening

THE WRITER.
yes

LAILA.
and in new york city

THE WRITER.
yes

LAILA.
of all places

THE WRITER.
right

LAILA.
and in 2011

THE WRITER.
yes

LAILA.
how could anyone do that to another person

THE WRITER.
exactly

LAILA.
a fellow human being

THE WRITER.
right

LAILA.

a brother essentially

if you look at life a certain

THE WRITER.

yes

LAILA.

and even worse

you love him

THE WRITER.

i

LAILA.

i mean

it's someone you care for deeply

–

stay right there

i have this really special

here

this special box

okay well actually it's just big and star shaped

and covered in gold glitter

so i guess it's not that special

but he'll be on a lot of drugs

THE WRITER.

yes

LAILA.

then it'll probably look like god

here let's fill it with

THE WRITER.

okay

LAILA.

goodies

okay this is our "butterball" bath bomb

THE WRITER.

does it smell like exploding turkey

LAILA.

no silly

it's filled with creamy cocoa butter

which helps moisturize because a bath

can actually dry out your skin

especially if too hot

and also it smells like vanilla and custard

let's give him two of those

THE WRITER.

okay

thank you

and what's that one

LAILA.

okay this one is our "exploding turkey" bath bomb

kidding

it's our "fizzbanger"

THE WRITER.

whoa

LAILA.

apple cinnamon bathtime fireworks

ooooh and this one is our "*ne* worry *pas*"

bergamot orange with a soy milk bonus

fizzle your worries away and send them down the drain

calming no matter how bad your day

hm

he could probably use some extra

i'll put in five

THE WRITER.

oh

that's a lot

LAILA.

sounds like your friend's life

not to mention face

was just rearranged

probably forever
don't think you can overdo the bath bombs
besides
they're on us

THE WRITER.

oh no no no that's not

LAILA.

now
let's celebrate his sexuality
as stereotypically as possible
they can beat him up
but they can't stop him from taking a rainbow bath after
right
right
now i've got a "think pink" bath bomb here
with tonka and neroli oil
said to induce euphoria
this one is called the "fairy ball"
need i say more
oh and this one is "all that jas"
as in jasmine
and also musical theatre

THE WRITER.

thank you
this is too

LAILA.

and last but not least
"sex bomb"
for when he's feeling better
just in case you want to blow his
brain
wink wink
reconnect
take a bath together

whoops
don't look now
but you're blushing
tucking a bunch of extra
scrubs and creams in there for

THE WRITER.

you are too

LAILA.

oh stop that
put your money away

THE WRITER.

no it's really

LAILA.

put that away

THE WRITER.

no
i'm sorry
i'm going to pay for the

LAILA.

i said put it away

–

listen
i know there's nothing i can say or do
that will actually make things better
but um
but

> (**LAILA** *hands* **THE WRITER** *the box.*)

Four Weeks After The Attack (Part 4)
March 15, 2011

THE ACADEMIC.
    the weirdest thing
    the fucking weirdest thing happened
    when i showed up to see that apartment
    met the realtor there
    i knew he could tell

THE WRITER.
    tell
    tell what

THE ACADEMIC.
    could tell what happened
    worse
    he could tell who i was
    he knew who i was

THE WRITER.
    how

THE ACADEMIC.
    i don't know
    the paper
    the blogs
    i don't
    –
    oh god
    my face must be all over the internet
    oh god
    oh god i feel

THE WRITER.
    listen
    why don't you just stay a while longer
    here

in your current apartment

THE ACADEMIC.

no no no

i just need to

i need a change of

my whole life is

THE WRITER.

or

you could

–

you are really gonna think i'm crazy

but you could

come stay with me

at my place

just for a while

just

on the couch

or

you can have my bed

i'll take the couch

–

THE ACADEMIC.

wow that's

i couldn't do that but

–

but that means a whole lot to

THE WRITER.

oh

yeah

forget i even

i didn't mean to

–

so

what'd you do today

THE ACADEMIC.

watched this terrible film

well i didn't even watch it

i listened to it

in the dark

that one with

ryan gosling and michelle

dawsonscreekwhatshername

the one everyone jizzed over when it

THE WRITER.

ohhh that break up porn

yeah

THE ACADEMIC.

exactly

they go through this break up and just

rip each other apart

i mean it actually turns violent

physically violent

i had to

i went to my room

curled up on the bed

turned off the lights

listened to it

tried to sleep

–

THE WRITER.

wait

did you cut your hair again

THE ACADEMIC.

yeah

THE WRITER.

but you just went

a week ago

THE ACADEMIC.

i know i

THE WRITER.

less than a

THE ACADEMIC.

wasn't happy i

THE WRITER.

how much do they

THE ACADEMIC.

like sixty

plus tip

THE WRITER.

sixty dollars

jesus does it come with

a hand job or

a free infant or something

you spent 120 dollars in a week on two haircuts and you

THE ACADEMIC.

it's all i can control

–

my face still looks like rocky balboa

and i have the same fucking syndrome

soldiers suffer coming back from war

what the hell do you want from

THE WRITER.

no i know

i'm sorry

i'm sorry

THE ACADEMIC.

no i know

me too

me too

–

THE WRITER.

you

THE ACADEMIC.

what

THE WRITER.

look great

your hair looks great

–

i walked down the street again last night

THE ACADEMIC.

what street

THE WRITER.

north 4th

between berry and wythe

the street where it happened

i keep going

did you know

the street lights

the whole block

they're all out

dark

THE ACADEMIC.

yeah i'm aware

it's the construction

all the new condos going up

city gets lax on streetlights until the people with money
move in

–

that night

you know what i remember thinking

walking down that block right before they

i remember it reminded me of that one summer night

when we were first

do you remember that one night
all the street lights on my block went out that night

THE WRITER.

yes
and i thought it was the taliban
but that not getting sleep
was a scarier prospect
so i put on vivaldi

THE ACADEMIC.

i said i would never fall asleep

THE WRITER.

but you did
i put on vivaldi and you did fall asleep

THE ACADEMIC.

he's a snooze
but most of all
i remember waking up that night and i know it sounds
so silly but
i could swear there was
something
next to the bed
next to my ear
breathing into it
saying

–

gonna get you

–

without actually saying it
i don't mean a dream
i mean a real thing
just next to me
breathing
waiting
waiting

for me
and i
i

–

–

–

> *(A sudden loud noise in the space – something falls. [Note: this should be a practical sound, not a recorded effect, and should be loud and abrasive enough to actually jolt the audience.]* **THE WRITER** *and* **THE ACADEMIC** *both jump and react verbally.* **THE WRITER** *starts to go and check on the sound – but then* **THE ACADEMIC** *starts to hyperventilate, heaving, sobbing, barely able to breathe. He tears and claws as* **THE WRITER** *tries to help him.)*

THE WRITER.

hey
hey hey hey
babe babe
i'm here
babe
look at me
look at me
try to relax
try to breathe
loosen this
listen to
feel my
listen to my
loosen
listen

> *(***THE ACADEMIC** *'s diaphragm and lungs loosen and take in some air. He gasps and gasps.)*

there we go
there you are

see
just a little co2
amazing what a little carbon dioxide can do for the
blood
right
and the blood in turn for the nervous
there we are
i'm right here
i'm here

—

  (Then a surprise: kissing.)

whoa um
is this

THE ACADEMIC.
please

THE WRITER.
okay

THE ACADEMIC.
please just
touch

THE WRITER.
okay

THE ACADEMIC.
me
no one has
has touched me since it
please just
touch

THE WRITER.
okay

THE ACADEMIC.
me

  *(***THE WRITER*** holds ***THE ACADEMIC.***)*

boy

—
girl
—
boy or girl
right before it happened
they asked me
"are you a boy or a girl"
but then
they didn't really mean "are you a boy or a girl"
they meant "are you a faggot"
do you think i should have said
"yes i am
and can we discuss it over dinner or something
because this street corner is cold"
do you think things would have gone differently
if i had tried and bought them a hot meal
and talked it over
they're afraid of anything different from them
or of what they see in me that maybe
they see in themselves
feel terrible for those kids
i should be angry right
but
mostly i feel worried
like any time they pop into my head i'm like
"oh i hope those teens who beat the shit out of me
turn out okay"
is that unhealthy

THE WRITER.
no
it's hopeful
hope is healthy
theoretically
—

come here you

–

i feel

THE ACADEMIC.

what

THE WRITER.

lucky

THE ACADEMIC.

for

THE WRITER.

you

here

–

THE ACADEMIC.

did you mean it

when you said

that i could stay with you

at your place

just for a while

THE WRITER.

of course i meant it

THE ACADEMIC.

maybe i will then

just for a while

just

on the couch

End of Play

CPSIA information can be obtained
at www.ICGtesting.com
Printed in the USA
BVHW040516110620
581028BV00006B/466

9 780573 706165